JAMIE'S STORY

Jamie's Story

KIM HARRY

Pegbag Publishing

Dedication
To my beautiful wife Michelle, long
suffering sister Mandy Moo and bestie
Lou
Thanks for always listening.

Special mention
Claire and Jo
Thanks for being my guinea pigs.

Jamie's Story

Kim Harry

ISBN: 978-1-5272-8965-9

Prologue

1996

'For God's sake Jimmy you're gonna kill her, she's only fifteen.'

The kitchen looked ransacked. It was full of trampled food and empty beer cans spattered with blood and bile. Jimmy loosened his hands from around his daughter Jamie's neck, only to give his wife Sheila another slap to the floor. As she lay there with her face pushed flat against the cold ceramic tiles, he grabbed her hair to lift her head, spitting his homophobic opinions back at her face.

'Keep out of it, Sheila, no daughter of mine is acting like a fucking bloke and humiliating this family all over the estate. If she's a dyke, then she's sick and needs it beating out of her.'

The wound on the back of his head was still pissing with blood from the toaster that her brother had thrown at him earlier. Jamie jumped on his back and began punching away at the raw flesh, hoping to do more damage or at least get him to pass out.

'Leave my mother alone, you drunken bastard, or so help me I'll kill you when you're sleeping.'

He swung her beaten body around to the front of him and held her in a headlock. 'Kill me, will you?' He began crushing her face into him with his military arms. 'You and that fucking wimp of a brother of yours haven't got the nerve. How the fuck you're my kids, I don't know. All those fucking army years and this is what I get out of life, wasters the fucking lot of you.'

He pushed her out of his way and cracked open a can of Special. He tottered about desperately rubbing his head. The stress headaches were getting worse without this added injury. He looked down at his wife and kicked her in the side.

'Sheila, get your lazy arse up and sort this mess out. It's a fucking pigsty.'

It took three attempts for Sheila to get to her feet; stumbling sideways as she tried to regain balance. He looked over to Jamie, who hadn't taken her eyes off her pathetic bully of a father. Her breathing now as heavy as his and every inch of her body ached.

'You, my girl, can get in that shed with your brother, and I don't want to see you for the rest of the fucking night—do you hear me?'

She planted her feet hard and folded her arms refusing to move, Jimmy gave his daughter a hard slap across her head, then grabbed her by the arm. He dragged her to the back of the house and down to the shed at the bottom of the garden. She tackled and kicked with the strength of a captured animal as he struggled to open the padlocked door. When it eventually fell open the glare from the light startled Michael, who was crouched in the corner with his face drowned in tears. His father looked at him in disgust.

'Stop your whinging, you woose—you're fourteen-years-old, that's nearly a man—what's the fucking matter with you?'

He shoved her rigid body into the tiny dark space and attempted to put the padlock back through the hook whilst holding the door shut with his knee. Jamie was pushing as hard as she could with her sore bruised limbs from the other side, hoping to gain their freedom.

'He's more of a man than you, you bastard.'

When the lock finally took hold, she cleared a part of the small window with her sleeve and watched as he went back to the house. They could see the shadow of him hitting their mother as her defenceless screams howled out across the neighbourhood. As always, nobody came to help and the night on the Welsh council estate was just the same as any other.

* * *

June 1982

They took Jimmy and the rest of the boys from the Welsh Battalion to St Carlos bay. They were there to attack Argentine positions in the south of the Island. The appalling conditions consumed many a well-polished soldier's boot as they trudged around in waterlogged sludge with feet freezing from the soak through. Twenty-four hours spent trying not to wallow in the swill was relieved only by the further orders to pack up their kit and march up the Sussex mountains to undertake their forward positions.

The kitbag was heavy enough before the weight of the clay became an extra unwelcome traveller. Each unsteady step threatened the burden causing it to slide down hindering its bearer as the straps impaled their muscle torn shoulders. The unsuccessful attempts to hitch the kitbags higher gave no relief and only slowed them down.

After travelling for about five miles, another cruel joke marred their attempts. They had been unsuccessful in reaching their target in time so the powers that be brought them all back. Their new mission would be to board the Sir Galahad and sail to Fitzroy taking with them supplies, army vehicles and ammunition.

They arrived at Bluff Cove, Fitzroy on Jimmy's daughter's second birthday, 8th June 1982. Behind the line of a faulty starting pistol, kicking up the chalk were soldiers eagerly waiting to get to safety. Several attempts had been made to get them off the ship, but still no passage to freedom. Plans were changed then re-made ignoring their vulnerability of being seen on the open sea it seemed. The landing craft that they so desperately needed to get them off the ship was in dire demand and in use elsewhere, and there was nothing they could do about it. Tempers frayed above restless feet as the sweat of nervousness overwhelmed each soldier exposed to the enemy's aircraft that would soon circle above.

It was becoming a beautiful cloudless day after a red dawn, and everyone on board prayed under their breath for the landing craft to arrive. They had to get off; they were easy targets. Soon their luck was to run out, and they felt it.

It took six long hours before the saviour's word was heard; it was their turn at last. High spirits were returning as the bustle of preparations began. Jimmy and the boys had been sitting amongst the ammunition boxes playing cards below deck. He had felt lucky and had bet his two-pound watch against his mate's expensive Rolex and won. As he walked away from them, strapping the watch to his hand with a winner's smile, the missiles hit.

Just for a moment, there was darkness. Two Mirage aeroplanes had attacked Sir Galahad and Jimmy was thrown across the deck as if he were weightless. As he blinked profusely for his sight to return, a deep roaring sound rang in his ears, urging him to make sense of what was happening. Amongst the orange air, he struggled to get to his feet. Through the haze, his focus zoomed in on the burnt bodies that were laid out before him. Twisted and mangled like surplus mannequin's in storage. As he tried to manoeuvre himself over them, he realised that he too was now on fire. The blast had caught the side of his face and his shoulder, but he was yet to feel any pain. As he quickly patted himself to extinguish the flames, a message came that they should get to the top deck and abandon ship. Panic was now getting harder to control. The smell of crisped flesh filled his nostrils as he stood in a line of smouldering soldiers, all helping each other to amble through the tiny door. Not long after they reached the top, another colossal explosion was heard, it was the ammunition and vehicles from below deck. Jimmy knew then that he was wearing a dead man's watch.

He managed to get on to the lifeboat and watched as the burning ship that was still taking lives destroyed the silent skyline. The screams of soldiers saying goodbye to their loved one's rose in the embers that floated into the sky. Jimmy could feel the heat getting closer again and a bout of panic emerged amongst the soldiers as they started to drift dangerously close, back to the burning ship. Some used their burnt hands as paddles, others used them to wave for attention to anyone that could help. Their plight was noticed by the pilots of the Sea King Helicopters. They had been scouring the open sea, winching up survivors away from the lick of the flames. They immediately hovered down to sea level to blow the lifeboats away to safety with the force from their rotor blades. The windswept faces of those on the lifeboat felt the sting of its force blow through them, inflating their uniforms and restricting their ability to move.

As the lifeboat drifted closer to shore, Jimmy jumped off, salting his raw burnt flesh. He waded through the icy water before losing his footing and falling to his knees. His attempts to get back on his feet were unsuccessful, so he frantically grabbed away at the sand and rocks finally crawling to safety.

The field ambulance service was waiting for the survivors. The carnage was such that the ownership of so many body parts would result in a lot of nameless soldiers going to their watery graves without the acknowledgement of their heroic demise. As Jimmy was lifted onto the trolley and taken to hospital, he knew then that his wounds would eventually heal, but his mind had been damaged forever. Death personified was etched on the inside of his eyelids. Things could never be the same again.

When the news got back to Wales that Great Britain and Argentina were now at war, families were desperate to hear from their loved ones. Jimmy's wife Sheila had been panicking ever since she saw Thatcher's sullen face standing outside 10 Downing Street reeling off the seriousness of the situation with her deep monotone voice. It had never occurred to her on the day that she waved him off in Southampton that she may never see his handsome face again. The attack on Sir Galahad was covered extensively by the BBC. The devastation was displayed in full colour with no holds barred. She clung to a slither of hope when the broadcast stated that only half of the Welsh Guards were on board. She convinced herself that he had been on the other ship, believing her gut instinct that he was safe.

This time her gut instinct was tainted. She rocked like a baby with her hand firmly covering her mouth when It was confirmed to her on the Friday that Jimmy had been one of the guards on board Sir Galahad and that he was now missing. At first, she refused to believe it and asked them to check their records again for any discrepancies. As the facts were read aloud to her for the second time, she could hear the words, but her heart wouldn't let her absorb their meanings. She tried to keep hopeful, hugging their baby close, and praying that he would be found alive. After receiving the word through friends that some wives had already been told that their husbands had died, Sheila flickered hope. This may be a good thing that he hasn't yet been found, maybe he's just lost, she thought. She still refused to believe that her Jimmy may be one of the statistics, as she could sense his soul alive around her.

When the call came through to say that he had been found, she fell in a slump to the floor. He was hurt, but he was alive. Her fear had eventually been lifted. She vowed from that day that she would take care of him and never looked back.

* * *

Chapter 1

2009

Jamie tried to ignore the constant beep of text alerts by putting her pounding head back under the pillow. With sandy eyes and a mouth as dry as a cracker, she lay there, motionless with a hint of awareness that the day had started without her. The sun beamed through the edge of the window blind, lining the white sheets with a criss-cross pattern heading for the eyes of a hangover.

Jewels, the lounge bar and nightclub that she owned was already busy preparing for the weekend. The deafening frequency of bottles and glasses shattering as they hit the recycle bin became a regular morning alarm to her living in the flat above. The slamming of doors by the whistling delivery drivers and the rolling of beer barrels up and down the pavements meant that she couldn't sleep in even if she wanted to.

During a well-earned yawn, the stale smell of last night's drinking session exhaled from her mouth. The flashbacks from her drunken antics made her cringe but gave no remorse. It had been her usual Friday night out in Cardiff, drinking copious amounts of alcohol with the girls, followed by downing shots and playing pool. As soon as the night gave fear of ending, fornicating with a total stranger and returning home alone would follow.

Last night she had had the pleasure of a straight, married, forty-something dressed as a St Trinian girl. Jamie hooked up with her in the chip shop queue on Caroline Street. She was out with a hen party and waiting for a takeaway to soak up the beer before attempting the taxi home. A drunken rendition of 'Sex on Fire' was wailed out when they began to out-sing each other. When Jamie finished, she pinched the girl's boater off her head and playfully refused to give it back. It became a game of cat and mouse as the chemistry between them mixed. The rest of the queue egged them on and joined in with the banter, causing the place to become overly boisterous. Much to the annoyance of the others in line, the stressed-out chip shop owner served them first simply to get rid of them.

After a short walk with their well-earned bag of chips, they landed themselves in a shop doorway, creating alternative ways to keep warm whilst hiding from the voyeurs behind the security cameras. This was a common occurrence for Jamie, and a habit too over-rehearsed to break.

At twenty-nine, she knew that commitment should be next on her agenda, but there was never enough time to pencil someone in, let alone promote them to the permanent ink. For now, nights out with the girls were her only commitment. When she was away from the club, all she needed was the company of a few good friends who would watch her back, and always be there with an alibi when asked.

The bedroom was a mess, as usual. The carpet that used to be green was now covered in coffee cups and rolled up bits of paper from the fall-out of a song she was half-heartedly working on. It had taken forever for her to learn the lyrics, and she had to perform it for a wedding party that weekend. She figured she could blag her way through with a bit of banter if her memory failed, so gave up for beer instead. The mess would have to stay there. She had no intention of wasting her day on housework; it would have to wait for a clear-headed approach.

Leaning over the side of the bed, she grappled around on the floor, hoping to find something to cover her tanned, almost athletic body. With one eye open and the other in squinting mode, she found a baggy t-shirt and a pair of beer-stained jeans. The t-shirt was way too feminine for her and not one of her own. This didn't matter, as long as it would join her in the kitchen for her coffee fix, that was all she needed it for. Its true owner would have been long gone and erased from her memory as soon as she sobered up so she couldn't ask to borrow it, even if she wanted to. Before making it to the kitchen, she was interrupted by shouting, bellowing through the hallway from the bottom of the stairs.

'Jamie—Butty—Are you awake?'

The shout came from Jamie's cellar hand, Beefy. He was a huge lump of a man with the voice of a coal miner, but he was also good at keeping the club in order if the bouncers were busy.

She shouted back at him, 'Well I am now,' she held her head at the sound of her own voice. 'Thanks, mate, I'll be down in a bit.' She had asked him to wake her when the delivery was over. She hated walking around the bar in the morning with the drivers leering at her. If they had been anywhere else than on her own property, she would have taken a swing at them for some of the crude suggestions they had given her in the past. She would always brush it off and not give them the satisfaction of replying, as she knew that any police trouble around a licensed bar was bad news. Avoidance was the best policy, and she knew she had an excellent team of staff to look after things for her.

There had only been one time that she felt the need to fire someone, and she did it in a second. Jewels was a place where people felt safe. It would welcome all walks of life to come through the doors. They knew that Jamie held no graces on who she regarded as lower than her. She treated the regulars like the family she never had, looking out for them all, and listening to their troubles. She had no time for jumped-up barmaids thinking they were better than anyone else.

The downstairs lounge bar at Jewel's was where she DJ'd on a Wednesday. There was not enough footfall in her little part of Wales to warrant opening the entire club, so it was open just for the mid-week crazies and her close-knit of regulars that couldn't stand the loud club atmosphere at weekends. She had taken on a young girl that had a lot of friends that attended her nightclub regularly, but when she gave verbal abuse to one of Jamie's favourite customers, she had to go.

It was the week before the Cardiff Pride Festival, and there were more people around than usual. She hired the girl to sit by the door and check the ID's of the younger customers, protecting her license from the underage drinkers. Jamie overheard her hurling abuse at Maud and telling her she wasn't allowed in. This type of prejudice had no place in Jewels, and Jamie told the girl to get her stuff and not come back. The fact that Maud was in her seventies with a purple punk hairstyle and leather chaps made no difference to the other club-goers or her.

She fitted in just like the rest of the odd bods, and Jamie had grown fond of the old bird. She would always buy her a drink and play her favourite song. Twenty minutes later Maud would push her way to the DJ booth and Jamie would know what was coming as she would yell at her through the plastic riot glass that was protecting her decks.

'Put YMCA on again,' she would shout.

'OK, Maud,' she would reply knowing full well that if she played it again the riot glass would come in handy. She would have to agree eventually though to stop the old bird from tapping on the glass and flashing her the finger.

Jamie always kept an eye on her when she came in and felt it her duty to look after her. Her son would turn in his grave if he knew that his mother was out alone. It was him that first brought her into Jewels three years ago.

They had 'popped in for one' as he would say, after the Pride march. One was never the case. His *one* would normally lead them to drink each other under the table.

The chemotherapy started last year, and everyone thought that he had beaten cancer, but back it came with a vengeance, leaving Maud without her son. Back then she would moan about his dress sense, complaining that he was too flamboyant to be walking the streets like that. But now, she would wear his chaps with pride. The purple punk hairstyle was one of his wigs. When his hair started falling out, Jamie bought it for him to cheer him up. Maud always wore it now. Maud wasn't her actual name, it was Carol. She used to drive around in an old wreck of a car and became 'Maud with the Ford.' But since she had her licence revoked because of poor eyesight, Jamie would make sure she stayed sober herself to drive her home if she ever came to the club. The hard exterior that Jamie showed to the public changed when she worked the lounge bar. She may have had a barrier around her own heart but gave it willingly to others when needed.

The kettle squealed its way to boiling point as she opened every cupboard door, searching for paracetamol for her headache. She eventually found them and took three, just in case. This was as reckless as she got with recreational drugs these days.

She sat at the breakfast bar trying desperately not to fall off the high-stool and pulled her laptop towards her. Every morning before planning her day, she would check her Facebook page and update her status. This was her way of keeping in touch with society and letting absent friends know that she was still alive. With her coffee threatening to spill in one hand, and the other hand now tapping away, she filled in her status box.

Jamie Taylor is... feeling like someone who went to sleep on a spin cycle and is now in serious need of an iron.

Perfect, she thought as she typed with a smile. That sounds exactly where my head is today after last night's binge session with the girls. She took another sip of her coffee and hit the down button to scroll through her friend's updates.

Blah Blah Blah—I don't know why I bother reading through this shit. Nearly two-thousand friends added, and I wouldn't recognise half of them if I saw them in the street, she thought as she continued to scroll down.

Mel is... in love and can't wait to see a certain someone.

This is the third girl this month and we're only halfway through, she thought. She shook her head, then recoiled her fingers away from adding a sarcastic comment. She would never tell someone she loved them without meaning it. It would have to be someone very exceptional to make her declare undying monogamy. As she continued to scroll, not really focusing on the screen, her eyes were averted to her brother's mobile and half a Kit-Kat bar at the end of the worktop just waiting to be eaten. Her brother was always leaving his phone behind. She pictured the scenario of him coming back in a while, throwing stuff around, trying to find it. She considered eating his chocolate just to teach him a lesson but couldn't be bothered to move.

Sam is...feeling like she's been eaten by a billy goat then shat out all over a cliff.

Now that is a fair statement, she thought. Her mind wandered, and she laughed out loud, remembering a blurry scene from the night before. 'Boom Boom Pow' she had sung as she tried to whack Sam over the head with a traffic cone. She recalled them stumbling home after her antics pissed as pants. Sam fell headfirst into something that resembled a pizza, garnished with carrots and swimming in alcohol. It had had regurgitation written all over it, and so did Sam. The thought had put her mind off eating the chocolate, and she could feel bile welling up in her mouth. She took a large swig of her coffee and it helped; she continued.

Julie is...wishing her mam and dad a Happy Anniversary.

She thought about her own parents, and how they had shared a volatile marriage for years. Too many times she had heard her mother cry herself to sleep and wake up the next day covered in bruises. She had spent her teenage years on a battlefield of arguments; not the best place to spend your adolescence.

As the pages drifted into mindless nonsense, she noticed the flashing icon of her 'Friend Request Box' this was usually a request from some faceless stranger trying to ogle the lesbian photos for kicks, so she held no expectations. Not this time. The friend request was from Heather Williams, nee Gardner. Jamie's eyes widened with surprise. She had thought of searching for Heather in the past, but nerves had always got the better of her. She hovered over the 'accept or reject' buttons as her heartbeat thumped with anticipation.

* * *

Jamie had known she was different from an early age. As a child, she was more interested in tying her brother's Action Man to a chair before abseiling him into a sandpit, than playing with dolls and prams. Her cute little dresses were always torn from climbing trees and her knees were constantly caked with blood. Mudpies and slugs were her favourite pass time along with searching for some worthy opponent to have a fight with.

In her first year of high school, she had the teachers baffled when looking for the little boy wearing a hoodie that was obsessed with vandalising the staff room. She was captured on the security cameras every time but still, the school had no idea it was her they were looking for.

At thirteen, she hit puberty and hated it. The monthly abuse of her boy-like body brought her down and embarrassed her terribly. She found the ritual of finding a different shop to steal sanitary towels from harder each time. She couldn't ask her mother as that would embarrass her even more. As the months went by and growth took hold, looking at herself in the mirror and accepting who she was to become added to her confusion. She hated that her shirts didn't fit right anymore but wearing a bra didn't fit in with her dress code either. It spent most of the time at the back of the wardrobe or being kicked around her bedroom floor.

School life was challenging, while the other girls were obsessing over boys and make-up Jamie was obsessing over the other girls. The immaturity of the boys and their playground lies meant that they were always spreading rumours to big themselves up to their mates. When the girls were upset, she made sure she was always there to pick up the pieces and to offer a shoulder to cry on. She became a good listener and always supplied a number of hugs of which she used to her own advantage.

Girls would be attracted to her, and it confused them as to why.

She was cute in a tomboy like way, with her jet-black hair, bright blue eyes and cheeky smile. As she grew into her teens, girls, as well as boys, would tease her purposely to get her attention and she encouraged every ounce of it. But disregarding the others, there was only one girl for her, and she knew it.

Chapter 2

1996

Decadent school days gave Jamie her playing field. Confident with her own sexuality but not with the way others perceived her, she kept her head down, only raising it to take in the view.

Heather had become a constant obsession for Jamie. She had formed crushes on many the unknowing girl in the past, but they would soon fade from her imaginative thoughts, or get side-lined by a prettier face, but not Heather. She was so different from Jamie. Her hair was the colour of fresh corn, and her skin flushed with the rapture of youth. Social status divided them, but not so obviously apparent on her part. Older in her ways, she was always the advocate for helping peers, and never one to victimise or gossip. Jamie admired that about her. She shared her obsession with most of the boys in her school, but this didn't faze her. She had convinced her-self that this was the year she would act on her impulses and put her charm to good use.

Jamie had decided to follow Heather home from school for the fourth time that week. It was the middle of May and the school term would be finishing soon with the summer holidays scurrying ever closer. This was her final year. She would be turning sixteen, dodging exams and looking for something resembling a job. With no rea-son to be anywhere, in particular, it would be harder to make up an excuse for following Heather around, so she figured that she needed to get in as much stalking time as possible.

Amongst a pack of dishevelled teenagers all fighting to get out of the school gate, she caught sight of Heather. The game was on and luckily for her, Heather had her best friend Abi alongside which would guaran-tee an easy walk home via the canal. The overgrown trees that framed the sides and the twists and turns of the makeshift path would make it easier for her to keep a safe distance away and not be noticed.

Keeping her head down, she scuffed along behind them, only looking up for brief seconds to make sure she still had the girls in her sight. The brogues she had commandeered from her brother had a hole in the bot-tom and she had covered it with the top of a cereal box. This had stopped her socks getting dirty but was no barrier for the tiny little stones of the canal path lodg-ing themselves between her toes. This wouldn't deter

Jamie though; the mission had begun, and she couldn't stop for a single second. She could cope with a bit of a limp—if it were worth it in the end, she thought. She watched Abi wave her goodbyes to her friend then walk up the path to her house just as she had hoped. Heather would have to continue the rest of the journey alone, or so she had thought.

With the sun breaking through the trees, Jamie squinted to keep Heather in her sight. She picked up her speed and without realising how close she was getting, her prey confronted her.

'I know you're following me,' Heather shouted. She didn't turn around, just kept on walking with her gaze firmly ahead.

At the same time, Jamie came to a standstill, feigning ignorance while her face bathed in a crimson glow. She didn't want Heather to think of her as some type of crazy stalker, even though she was.

'You can catch me up—I won't bite.' Heather shouted louder this time. Jamie liked that comment. She had a bit of a vampire eroticism thing going on in her head at the time and thought it to be quite apt as she avidly seized the moment.

'Wait up then!' Jamie nervously sprinted to join her. She could feel her doubts clinging to her as her legs got heavier, weighing her down with each stride. This was such a crazy idea even for her, she thought.

They walked for a while in teenage silence. She had imagined this moment so many times in her head it was almost like a memory. The plan was to act all cool and sophisticated, but now the uncontrollable shake in her legs had got the better of her. When Heather spoke, she tried to listen intently, but the more she talked the more she felt as though she was walking on sinking sand, wriggling nervously to stay afloat.

'You're Jamie—right' Heather said with a smirk.

She didn't have time to think of a response and hoped that she would just open her mouth and reply with something clever and witty like she normally did.

'Yeah, that's my name don't wear it out.' She cringed as the words fell from her lips, knowing that she had just thrown away the chance to say something that would really make an impression. Embarrassed by her choice of childish humour she bowed her head and shamefully tried to regain some decorum. 'I am so sorry; I don't know where that came from—can we start again?'

Heather opened her mouth as if to speak, but Jamie jumped in first.

'Yes—it's Jamie—you're right, but before you ask, I wasn't following you. I just thought it would be nice to go this way for a change. We just happen to be going in the same direction, that's all.' Jamie tried to sound confident, but she could hear herself rambling on and couldn't seem to control it, digging herself deeper and deeper into absurdity. Heather's facial expressions made it known that she wasn't convinced. She enjoyed watching Jamie try to explain herself before saving her with an overdue sarcastic reply.

'Ah, right—of course, you were. I thought you lived on the other side of the estate. That's got to be over a mile difference.'

This was, in fact, true, and it took Jamie an extra half an hour to get home from school when following Heather took priority. Her mother hadn't seemed to notice though, and her father would be too busy looking at the bottom of a pint glass to worry about what time Jamie or her brother strolled in.

'Yeah—I do—but sometimes I just like to think when I'm walking, so I take the long way home.' She smirked as she was quite impressed with herself for that reply.

'Think—walk and stalk more like!' Heather giggled, and her nose did that scrunched up thing that Jamie loved so much.

'It's OK, it doesn't bother me, at least you're not whistling or flicking elastic bands at me to get my attention like the boys do.' She was used to a lot of attention and accepted it with confidence. 'They think it impresses me, but it just makes them look childish and I'm not into that.'

Heather was right. It was stalking, and that's exactly what she'd been doing since she first noticed her. She had spent most of her time at school hiding around corners just to get a glimpse or bumping into her accidentally on purpose, just for a sorry to be exchanged. The fact that now they had had a conversation would give Jamie a buzz for weeks to come. Jamie replied, feeling a little more at ease with herself now that the ice had broken.

'So, what are you into?'

Heather stopped dead in her tracks and pulled Jamie towards her. With a gentle smile, she whispered, 'You.'

After her announcement, she took a few steps backwards, ran into the tunnel and waited under the bridge. Jamie felt frozen to the spot. She didn't know whether to follow her or just stand and stare, totally gob-smacked. Had she understood her reply correctly? Did she mean how it sounded or was she joking around to add to the embarrassment? The small tree branch she had been nervously peeling the bark off was almost bare, and she was twirling it around her fingers like a baton. Jamie couldn't hold the suspense any longer and skulked her way a few steps cautiously towards her.

'Did you really mean it?' She waited impatiently for an answer and carried on shouting over to her, 'If you're trying to make fun of me, I will have to throw this stick at you. I don't want to as it's taken me so long to peel it, but I will—I mean it,' she jokingly waved it at her.

Laughter echoed from inside the tunnel. She had made Jamie wait long enough.

'How do you think I know where you live, you're not the only one that can follow someone home, you know, I just made a better job of keeping it a secret than you did?'

Jamie had wondered why she hadn't slapped her by now, as the stalking had become a lot more frequent. As she slowly absorbed what Heather had said, she realised it was true. She hadn't had to try too hard to find her recently.

Jamie hadn't expected the welcome response and was still a little dubious as to whether her intentions were honest. Was it a cruel trick or the start of something beautiful? Either way, she would not run away from it and moved in closer.

'OK, so I won't be throwing this stick at you then,' Jamie said with a smirk as she entered the tunnel.

They sat down with their backs against the wall, both picking at the remaining tree bark nervously. The smell from the damp moss that covered the canal hung in the air as the need for a break in the silence was imminent.

Heather kept her eyes focused down. Even she was feeling a little less brave now.

'I had hoped that you would make the first move,' she said as she bumped shoulders with her. 'You always seem so confident at school.'

Jamie wanted to reply but couldn't find the words. She was in awe of the girl sat next to her and the art of conversation evaded her when it came to Heather Gardner. This blond, green-eyed beauty had been her ultimate goal for the summer, and now she was waiting for her response. 'I was — just waiting for the right moment, I didn't want to seem too pushy.' she murmured coyly.

'Right moment!' Heather laughed 'You've been following me around all term I was beginning to think that you were teasing me.'

Heather slid her hand across the floor towards Jamie, their fingers barely touching. Jamie could feel it shaking as she wrapped her fingers around it. Heather lifted her head for the first time, and the eye contact between them was unmistakable. Jamie knew then that Heather was serious.

'I do like you, Jamie. I don't really know why myself. All I know is thinking about you makes me smile.'

Jamie helped Heather to her feet, her hands still sticky from the tree sap. Whilst taking an intake of breath, she made the conscious decision to kiss her. Keeping hold of Heather's hand and gearing it towards her own waist, she closed her eyes and hoped that gravity would force them together. The lingering and waiting for Heather's soft lips to be placed on hers, had Jamie shaking hysterically. She knew that she wanted this and yet, the anticipation was arduous. Heather was already sixteen and not like the other girls always teasing her and playing games. This was real, she was real. Jamie had kissed a few girls, daringly, and even boys in the past, but it never really meant anything to her. She had just used them to get drunk with and to fit in, be part of the gang. Nothing had ever affected her like this.

Jamie could hear her own heartbeat drumming loudly in her ears as she leaned forward. The hesitancy of their first encounter was broken by the sweet taste of Heather's full-blooded lips. Slowly they had found each other, small delicate kisses at first, had the girls trembling in each other's arms and yet each kiss so precise in its intention. She tried desperately not to lose balance when the warmth of Heather's tongue engulfed her and drained her of breath. No longer would she be able to keep her obsession a secret as it would be written all over her face. She wanted to open her eyes to make sure she wasn't dreaming, but as their emotions washed over them, the moment paralysed her.

They held each other for a little while, Heather's long hair draped Jamie's shoulder as they both stood in silence bathing in their conduct. The warm afternoon was coming to a close, and they both knew that they should be getting home.

'Are you OK?' Jamie held Heather's face in her hands. 'What we did—was that OK?'

She pulled Jamie tighter and gently placed a kiss on her cheek.

'Do I look like I'm complaining? It was more than OK.'

Jamie exhaled the breath she had held nervously while waiting for the answer as Heather started to move away.

'I had better go, I don't want to, but my parents will send out a search party for me if I'm not home soon.' She watched as Jamie's face disheartened. 'I'm not putting you off—look, can I meet you here after school tomorrow?'

'Of course, yeah, I think I could manage that—and maybe I won't walk behind you this time.'

As Heather started to run home, she shouted back, 'I'll hold you to that.'

The afternoon's events repeated themselves in her over-thinking mind as she began her long walk home. She had finally got close to Heather after months of what she thought was secret surveillance. Whatever happens next will be a fresh experience, but that moment they had shared she would never forget. She decided that she would up her game tomorrow and lose the shyness. Try to act more casual around her.

As she entered her street, the usual faces were out hanging off railings and playing Kerby across the busy roads. Annoying drivers with footballs bouncing off their cars would swear at the kids and threaten to grass them up to their parents. As she looked around at the gangs of kids on the corners her first instinct was to tell the world about her conquest but knew she couldn't, she must keep this secret close to her heart, where the need for her began.

Chapter 3

Before she had time to put the key in the door, she could hear her parents arguing through the living room window. She paused for a few seconds, debating whether to turn back. The growling of her stomach changed her mind, so she entered as quickly as possible. She ran straight upstairs to her room, safely avoiding the cross-fire. After staring blankly out of her window over to the quarry, she switched on her CD deck and blasted out 'Weak' by Skunk Anansie to drown out the conflict.

Her room was covered in posters so not a single piece of torn wallpaper or black flaky mould could be seen. If any did start to eat its way through, she would simply change the poster, and this worked for her.

The faces of Nirvana, Oasis and the Manic Street Preachers imposed her walls along with Elvis and of course Jodie Foster. The ceiling had a lot of erotic posters of Madonna but was mainly covered with a massive poster of the new band Spice Girls. She hated that 'Wannabe' song and didn't think they would be around for long, but they were good to look at, so she kept it. She also didn't give a shit that Take That had split up—but made out that she did to her friends in school. It devastated a lot of them, bursting into tears in the middle of lessons. She found it ridiculous but wouldn't tell them that, instead, she would put her arm around them to comfort them. This gave her a sense of being needed, and she loved it. As soon as she was able, she would steal stuff for them on a Saturday morning from Woolworths. She found it easy stealing from there as the shop was on a hill with two floors and two separate exits. She would raid the junk jewellery stand downstairs, then make her way to the escalator. It would take the brief journey to shove them into her jacket pocket and zip them away before exiting on the top floor. It worked every time.

Jamie's bedroom was always cold, even in the summer. The only fire in the house was in the living room. When she was younger, she would bundle up her clothes in the mornings and take them downstairs to change into. But as soon as puberty came along, she was upstairs shivering in her tiny room, dressing as fast as she could. On the weekends she often slept fully clothed, so she wouldn't have to change the next day.

A lot of her friends had central heating, but she had to make do with putting heavy coats on her bed to keep her warm in the winter. The windows would completely freeze up on the inside and leave pools of water dripping on to the floor, or on her when defrosting. It was only a small room, and she had to put the bed under the window as this was the only place it would fit. Her carpet didn't reach to the walls and the bare floorboards gave her splinters. She covered some of it with a few old carpet tiles that she found at the tip. They were all different colours, but she thought it looked funky like that.

The arguing continued downstairs, so she turned the stereo dial to full. She would not let it get her down. She was smiling uncontrollably and still couldn't believe what had happened. Her time spent with Heather was exactly how she had imagined it to be, nothing would knock her off this cloud.

As she jumped around the tiny room, she felt the floorboards creak in time with the music. She leapt onto her bed and lay there staring at the ceiling. So where do we go from here? She wondered.

1996 had its share of lesbian and gay characters on television. Pop stars were jumping out of the closet at every given opportunity it seemed, so she was totally aware of what was happening to her. Still, to be openly gay at nearly sixteen was going to be something she might have to approach with caution. She had plucked up enough courage to step into the water a couple of times but had no idea how to tread it, let alone swim. Maybe now that she had someone she could share her emotions with, things would feel easier, she thought. But as clued up as she may have liked to think she was, she knew that there were a lot of questions that couldn't go unanswered.

Heather had a boyfriend, and everyone knew this. They used to strut around the school together like Barbie and Ken. He was a bit of an arsehole; she thought as he always used to glare at her when they walked past. She wondered if that had been anything to do with Heather liking her. Maybe he had guessed and had a touch of jealousy, she thought.

Her mind was all over the place now. How could it have been possible for Heather to have liked her all this time and her not pick up on it? Why did she still go out with him if he was not what she wanted? She mulled things over and wondered if she had read it wrong. Maybe I'll have to share her? She thought.

She then imagined the worst-case scenario that Heather would change her mind and pretend that it had never happened. She couldn't bear to think of how she would handle the rejection. It would be so hard sitting in the same classroom as her and not be able to get close enough to touch her.

So many questions and concerns for her head to process, but the way she was feeling at that moment meant that none of the answers really mattered. She had kissed the girl that she had stalked forever, and no one could delete that from her memory. Her head then pictured other scenarios of them both together, but the images were soon erased by the banging on her door from Sheila, her mother. She jumped at the invasion and turned her music off.

'Jamie, can you come downstairs love and help me clean up? Your father threw his dinner again. He didn't get that driver's job he went for this morning, they rang and told him. He's really upset.'

He probably breathed on them. Or maybe they could tell how many beers he had had the night before, she thought. His feelings were always Sheila's only concern. How about how everyone else was feeling?

They would all have to keep out of Jamie Senior's way now for at least a week or a backhanded slap would surely be on the cards. She thought for a few minutes of her family and the reaction she would get from her dad if he ever found out. She had been up to much worse than this over the past couple of years, and in comparison, what had happened between her and Heather was mild. But that was just destructive behaviour. This would be different.

He hated queers because of his catholic upbringing and mocked everything that didn't conform to the norm. As long as she was careful, no one needed to know. This was her philosophy for most of her antics. Just keep a low profile and don't get caught, she thought. Her younger brother Michael would always get a good slice of his anger, and this worried her. Her father would mentally torture him just to show he was the bigger man.

Michael was just as handsome as Jamie. He kept himself to himself, and the few friends he had were a lot older than him. His dark looks made him seem like the moody type, and that's how he liked it. The other kids in his class didn't seem to understand his off the wall ways, and he found them too immature for his way of thinking. He was also off the rails and rebelling. Like Jamie, he was smoking a lot of cannabis and drinking too much. This was the only way that living in this family would deem bearable for them on some days. The constant arguing and their father's drink dependency was taking its toll on the complete family, and only the ones inside the circle seemed to know about it.

Jamie crept down the stairs and reluctantly picked up the smashed plate and bits of food in silence. It had scattered across the kitchen and living room doorway and by the way it had landed you could tell that he had probably thrown his plate directly at her mother in the kitchen, but fortunately for her, it didn't quite make it all the way.

Jamie Taylor Senior was not a tall or muscle-bound man, but one punch from him would send a man flying. He knew how to handle himself and certainly had more strength than he was showing on the outside. Lying in his chair now fast asleep made him oblivious to the commotion he had just caused. He revelled in the fact that all the family were living in fear of him. He would just live his life how he seemed fit and make everyone else's life a misery in the process.

From her knees, Jamie looked up at her mother with total frustration. She was bathing a cut on the side of her face where an escaped piece of flying crockery must have hit her. She winced with every dab of the cloth.

'Don't look at me like that Jamie, you know there's nothing I can do about it.'

Her mother's voice was softer than a whisper whilst keeping her eyes on her husband as not to wake him. Sorry was a word from the past. His troubled mind no longer held any remorse. Everything she said to him was misconstrued giving reason to beat her. All the love they had once shared was questioned by them both. She would have hell to pay if he knew that it wasn't just his wife cleaning up after him, so Jamie put the pieces in the bin outside, then quickly washed her hands. She grabbed herself a box of cereal from the cupboard and started ramming them into her mouth whilst taking a breath to talk in between.

'I'm going out Mam, I can't stay here and listen to his snoring. When he wakes up, he will have forgotten what has happened and head off back to the pub, so just keep out of his way until then OK,', she tipped her head back and poured the rest of the cereal down the back of her throat. 'I love you, Mam.'

Chapter 4

November 1979

Come on, Jimmy! Sheila paced back and forth by the window, waiting for her soldier to arrive. She pulled back the green velvet curtains and craned her neck as far forward as she could to get a look at the cars entering the street. The typical Welsh weather had steamed up the windows and made it impossible for her to distinguish a car from a taxi, but she stood firm. This was not the first time today as she had spent the damp raw morning underneath the one-bar electric heater used to de-mist the bathroom mirror. This was the only mirror with enough light for her to put her makeup on and get herself ready for Jimmy. After putting on her new red velour sports top with the white zip, she had spent hours manipulating her blond Farrah Fawcett hair to curl away from her face just how Jimmy liked it. She had bought the outfit just to welcome him home, and she knew that she looked good in it. The bold colours made her feel empowered, and that was what she needed right now. I know I can do this, she thought.

The longer she waited for Jimmy to arrive, the more her empowerment faded. The knots in her stomach had turned to boulders, and she stumbled to remember what she had planned to say. They had been dating for nearly a year and although he had spent a great deal of it at the army training regiment in Surrey, she was sure she knew him well enough to anticipate his reaction, or so she hoped. Maybe I won't tell him just yet, she thought. With restless feet, she made it to the hallway and opened the front door to look outside. Still no sign. It took all her strength from her tiny body to close it again from the pounding wind. Her eyes had become blood-shot from the heavy mascara and she had bitten one of her fingernails down to the quick. She was still unde-cided. No, it has to be today, she thought, he'd guess something was wrong and that would make things a lot worse.

Their time apart was heart-rending for both of them. They had spent most of his trips on leave horizontal in the back of his dad's Cortina, and a lot of the time it had got too intense too quickly to play it safe.

The taxi arrived surging through the concave puddles and she had made up her mind. I have to tell him I can't do this alone.

Mumbling voices had her fumbling to open the door. He was home, back in Newport safe.

Biting the inside of her cheek, she waited impatiently as he paid the taxi driver.

'Jimmy, hurry love, you'll be soaked through.' He bounded up the path, shaking his wet body before dropping his kit bag in the hall and grabbing her tightly for a kiss. She could feel the curl in her hair drop with the damp as droplets of rain fell from his hair onto her perfectly made-up face. She led him quickly by the hand through the door of her parents' modest semi-detached and thanked god that they were out for the day.

'Christ, I've missed you, girl, you look like an angel.'

Sheila draped her hands around his neck and kissed him again.

This was the welcome home he needed. He was only seventeen when he signed up for the Welsh Guards and already had the makings of a good soldier. When their lips could kiss no more, she turned her back to him and guided his hands around her, pressing them against her stomach over her high-top jeans. She took a deep breath and thought this was as good a time as any.

'Jimmy, you know how we talked about starting a family someday, well...' She was nervous about turning around to see his reaction, but she needn't had been as his smile said it all. 'You're not ...'

Sheila nodded and bit away nervously at her already bleeding finger as she watched her Jimmy display a mixture of emotions ranging from confusion to happiness and back again in the space of seconds.

It was his turn to pace the floor as he started making immediate plans for them and the baby in his head. He loved Sheila, and they had talked about getting married and starting a family someday, but was it too soon? He paused for a second and turned to face her. She was his everything from the second they had met at the roller disco in town to the time he told her he was leaving for Surrey. That night had been spent wiping away tears from them both.

'Wait now, you're not having me on are you, to see what I'd say like?'

Sheila shook her head. It was all he needed. He stood in front of her and held her hand. After getting on one knee, he looked up at her now crimson face. 'I know I haven't got a ring or anything, but it would make me the happiest man alive if you would marry me, Sheila.'

She accepted without hesitation, and her fears were instantly shelved. She jumped on top of his sodden body and held his face in her hands. 'Yes Jimmy, of course, it's yes.'

They kept the pregnancy a secret and had a quick wedding in the registry office. Just after Christmas Jimmy left to finish his training while Sheila began house hunting by bus with her friend Sal. She would know where to start with this for sure. They had met at school and were more like sisters, always in and out of each other's houses and enjoying life together.

'So why the rush to get married. I don't understand I thought you wanted the big fairy tale deal, not a quickie up the Manor.' Sal put the money in the slot for the bus ride and eyed up the driver upon entrance. As the driver pulled away the girls scowled as they lost their balance climbing the chewing gum ridden stairs. The bus was full, but they managed to squeeze into a seat at the back and Sal started rummaging through the pockets of her plastic mac for her cigarettes.

'It's not like you're up the duff or anything, is it?' She lit up a fag and offered one to Sheila, but she declined. 'Oh my god, you are, aren't you—it all makes sense now? You never say no to a fag.'

Sal's voice was as loud as the bright orange jumpsuit she was wearing, and the old couple in front turned around in their seats to offer a disgusted glance.

'Oi you two, it's got nothing to do with you she's old enough to do what she wants to so keep your nosey beaks out.' They turned back around as if they were going to anyway despite being waved in the face by Sal and her Embassy No 6. She nudged Sheila's arm then flicked ash over the old man's jacket, 'That told them.'

'Only you could get away with that on a bus full of people,' she whispered. 'Yes, I am up the duff as you so lovingly put it, but we haven't told anyone yet so keep your lips zipped, yeah.'

'Why so secretive? I can't see Jean and Brian having a problem with it they would stand by you I'm sure?'

'No, it's not my parents, its Jimmy's. They are devout Catholics, always advocating the sanctity of marriage and family values. They hated the fact we didn't have a church wedding, but I'm too far gone to wait for all of that palaver to be arranged.'

'Well, I never, little Sheila's been a naughty girl. That's the last time you have a go at me for entertaining the boys.' She gave Sheila a heavily lashed wink. 'So, when is lover boy back home then—or is he leaving everything for you to sort out?'

She looked down at her growing waistline and rubbed it tenderly. Jimmy had finished his training and had started living life as a soldier. She was proud of him. He had looked so smart in his uniform the last time she saw him, with his cropped black hair and ice-blue eyes. She had also noticed how much his body had developed since they had started dating. He now had a muscular frame, and his seventeen-year-old baby-face had been replaced with the look of a soldier.

'He'll be serving in Northern Ireland soon, so I offered to take on everything. I'm not completely useless. I've saved up some money and if I can just find us some-where that isn't full of damp and within our budget, we'll be fine.'

Sal wasn't convinced, but she didn't want to show Sheila that. She was worried about her friend and was willing to help her in any way that she could. She stood up to ring the bell and purposely knocked off the old lady's hat before apologising sarcastically and pulling Sheila to her feet.

'OK, Mrs James Taylor, let's find you a palace shall we.'

After a month of sifting through adverts and following leads from people who knew people, she was still no closer to finding anywhere half decent. Her body was growing too, and she was tired of all the rushing around. The money that she had scraped together was only enough for the baby things that they needed, and time was running out for the rest. When she got home from town after looking at cots with her mam, she was fit to drop. Jean went to the kitchen to the put the kettle on and when she returned Sheila was still sat on the settee in her coat, bags in hand, too tired to do anything else.

'I can't look at you like this anymore, Sheil, you're my daughter and I think you should stop all this traipsing around and raise the baby here. I've spoken to your dad, and he said he's happy for you both to move in—till you get something sorted like.' Her mum took Sheila's coat, placed it over the chair and put the shopping away.

Sheila was too tired to disagree with her this time and fell asleep on the settee watching crackerjack on the TV. Her body needed the regeneration time, and she wasn't going to argue. Jean always seemed a quiet and reserved character but was as stern as brass when it came to protecting her daughter. She was not a woman that would shy away from saying how she felt, so with Jimmy not around she felt she had to step in with a solution.

'Brian, get on that phone to Jimmy and tell him she's staying here. He can stay here too when he comes home from leave, but I'm not having her left alone when he goes to Ireland. Tell him it's just not fair on her. And Brian, make sure he doesn't talk you out of it. This is happening, and that's final.'

Sheila threw the coat over the top of her sleeping daughter and kissed her head.

* * *

When little Jamie was born, Jimmy held on to her as if she were made of china. Her eyes reflected his entire future. His memory of an unstable upbringing caused by his father's inattentiveness made him want the closeness even more. That man had been the master of excuses, always at the steelworks or down the pub playing cards and drinking his wage packet away. Jimmy hardly remembered seeing him as a child. He had not wanted the same for his little girl, but unfortunately for him, his career with the Welsh Guards was taking him away from his family in the same way, albeit with better intentions. He knew that getting a job closer to home would have been the answer, but career opportunities in the small Welsh town of Newport were dwindling. It was no longer a time where you could pick and choose on the employment front. For as long as he could remember, his dad had told him he should follow in his footsteps and get a job at Llanwern Steel, but now things were changing. With the past strikes causing uncertainty of a future, the men that had thought they had jobs for life were falling. Redundancies were a new phase, and Thatcher's dole queue was getting bigger.

House hunting had been harder than they had imagined. The waiting lists for council houses were getting longer due to the right-to-buy schemes but they bided their time and eventually picked the keys up for a council house on an estate close to Sheila's parents. It needed a lot of work doing to it, but it was theirs.

'Put the baby back in the pram, Sheila, I want to carry you over the threshold.'

As Jimmy picked her up, she felt safe in his arms until he bundled her through the door, banging her feet on the door frame.

'Steady, these shoes were on sale in Top Shop I don't want them scuffed.' He put her down and went back out to get the pram.

'Oh, Jimmy, we are going to be so happy here, the three of us, and as soon as you finish with the Welsh Guards we can really start living like a proper family.'

Jimmy just smiled. The same way he always did when he didn't want Sheila to see the worry on his face. He had tried looking for work, but there was nothing around.

'Hey, let's not get above ourselves yet Sheila, we don't know when that will be, remember I told you it takes a while to sort out. It could be ages before I get out of the service.'

He had decided to stay with the Welsh Guards without telling Sheila. Coming home on leave to her parent's house had felt restrictive, and he wanted out. Admittedly, they were buying things for the baby and only asking for minimal keep, but he felt as though he was receiving handouts. At least he was getting a regular wage in the Welsh Guards, and it made him feel more of a man.

They furnished the house with a loan from the Prudential, and her mam was secretly topping up the gas and electric meters and paying Rediffusion for the telly. Life was OK for a while until the coal mine Sheila's dad had been working at his entire life closed under the Tory government. Jean was inconsolable when she broke the news to Sheila on the phone. She wasn't worried about how it would affect them; they had lived a good life, but she knew that her daughter needed her help and would find it hard to manage.

'Mam, of course, I understand, you have to think of you and Dad for a change. We'll be OK Jimmy will be back from Northern Ireland soon and then things will look up.' The silence on the other end of the phone spoke volumes. Her mother had lost all faith in Jimmy, and Sheila knew it.

'Listen, you've done enough already, and it's about time I stood on my own two feet...'

Jean interrupted by hitting the nail firmly on the head.

'Sheila, you don't seem to understand love, we are going to have to move away as well for your dad to find work. Mining is the only thing he knows. There's nothing around here for him, he's already looked.'

Standing on her own two feet would be hard without her mother around to babysit when she did her couple of hours cleaning. They were also no longer in the position to help their daughter financially as they needed every penny to survive themselves. She knew that Sal would help her out as much as she could, but it was Jimmy that she needed to support her now and he was still so far away.

As the months went by, Sheila missed the support of her parents living so close. She no longer had them to fall back on, and as the payments increased on the loan, it made it harder for her to keep on top of things. The council rent was a lot more than she was paying her mother for her keep, and the money that Jimmy was sending home seemed to get less and less.

* * *

Northern Ireland was far from embracing peace. The segregation of religion had people throwing petrol bombs into their neighbour's gardens for nothing more than a hint of gossip. It filled the air with hate and fear against the British army, causing Jimmy the need for distraction. He was drinking hard and wasting his money with his battalion to take his mind away from the job in hand. They played cards for money to pass the time between shifts, but the urge to win was giving him a gambling habit. The more he gambled, the more he lost. He felt as though he was turning into his father and found himself writing more IOU's than letters home; leaving Sheila with the hardship that his own mother had to endure.

Jamie was growing out of her clothes at an unmanageable rate and crawling around getting into mischief. The repairs on the house were also getting out of hand. There had been a leak in the upstairs toilet, and it had flooded the kitchen cupboard below; the sewage ruined all the wedding photos and the memories of Jamie's birth.

Visits back home were few, and when he did return, he spent most of his time down the pub, washing away the thoughts of Northern Ireland. He would never tell Sheila what had gone on there and had always been the type of man to keep his problems to himself. He had missed his daughter and felt guilty for not giving her the life he would have wanted her to have. They looked so

much alike, and Sheila welcomed that when he wasn't
around.

She was still immensely proud of her husband and
when she had the chance for a trip to London to watch
her Jimmy Guardsman James Taylor trouping the colour
for the queen; she jumped at it.

* * *

It had started as a day to forget the mundane troubles
of a failing economy and a day to be proud of your coun-
try. Some of the soldier's wives couldn't hold back their
tears constantly crowing of how proud they were of their
husbands marching alongside the queen.

When the procession was over, Sheila waited at the
gates in the queue behind the other wives. A disgruntled
ex-soldier had fired blank gunshots, so the police were
keeping an extra diligent check on the crowds slowing
up the procession. The weather was warm, and the baby
was becoming restless, throwing her teddy-bear out of
the pram time and time again for her poor mother's
aching limbs to crouch down and pick it up.

'Jamie it won't be long my darling we will see daddy
soon.' She wiped her beautiful girls' rosy cheeks with a

tissue from her pocket and before standing unwillingly caught the conversation from two wives in front.

'It's disgusting how that Jimmy Taylor carries on. He's owed my Reg £20 for three months now. He said he needed the money to visit a sick relative who was having a life-threatening operation. Operation—my left foot. He drank it away as soon as he had it Reg said.'

They then discussed whether they believed it to be a lie, which under her breath Sheila regretfully acknowledged it was. She knew then that Jimmy had an even bigger problem than she had first thought. She was about to stand when the other woman continued.

'I pity his poor wife. Not only has he been gambling and drinking his money away, but according to my John, he had also been a regular visitor to the brothel behind St. Mary's.'

This broke Sheila, and instead of joining in with the further celebrations of the day, she took the next train home.

On returning from Southampton, she put the baby to bed and sat with a bottle of Jimmy's whiskey in the front garden. It had been a beautiful summer and the residents on the estate were all sat out doing much the same. Sheila wasn't there for the enjoyment though. The more she drank, the more she cried. The future she had seen for herself was in the gutter. She was only twenty-one and while the other girls her age were taking secretarial courses and out enjoying themselves at Scamps and the Stowaway club; she was on her own with a baby, a cheating husband and no money. The gossip had broken her. It was so apparent that a neighbour had heard her wailing and came over to help her back into the house. He was also three sheets to the wind and after a tearful heart to heart, one thing led to another.

When Jimmy came home for the weekend, she made up an excuse regarding why she had left the parade so early. She couldn't bring herself to ask him about the women and their gossip. In her mind she had got her revenge in a moment of madness on the kitchen table, so was willing to try again.

When he left to go back to Northern Ireland, she was glad in a way. She had had enough with the pretence and regretted trying to patch things up. He had spent most of the time at the bookies or down the pub. She hated the life that she was only half-sharing with him and harboured thoughts about leaving him.

She tried her best to pull herself together and got a cleaning job where she could take the baby along. She budgeted the extra money she had coming in and thought that maybe she could survive being a single parent. But two months later, her plans changed again. After a bout of sickness, she found out she was expecting another child. There was no way she could bring up the two on her own, so she decided she would have to remain a soldier's wife and give her marriage another try.

* * *

In March 1982, Michael was born. He was her beautiful baby boy clothed in Jamie's hand-me-downs. The debts of menial living had been piling up around her, and they were struggling with another mouth to feed. When Jimmy came home on leave, she gave him an ultimatum. She couldn't live this way any longer and told him that if things didn't improve, she would move to England and live with her parents. He was full of apologies for his lack in providing for his family and begged her to give him another chance. He was soon to be stationed in the Falklands to police the island, so he made her a promise that when he returned, he would get his act together.

They spent that night like old times, wrapped in each other's arms. The next morning, she begged him not to go. She was a month behind on the rent, and the woman from the Prudential had been knocking on the door every day to collect what they owed to them on the loan. Sheila had felt so ashamed that she had taken to hiding behind the furniture so not to be noticed if they started peering in through the window. Making sure that the baby didn't cry and expose her was an arduous task. The embarrassment of the situation if he ever started screaming his lungs out was worse than anything she had ever experienced. She didn't want to do this on her own any longer, but he assured her it would only be for a short time.

Jimmy was adamant that he was joining the first battalion of Welsh Guards on their journey to the Falkland Islands and wanted Sheila to come to Southampton with him to wave him off. She tried to defer him by making excuses that she didn't want to take the babies all that way, as it would be too unsettling for them. The real reason being she didn't want to bump into the other wives or accept their false sympathy. Jimmy insisted and went behind Sheila's back to ask her mother to have the babies for her overnight. He had a sick feeling in his stomach and needed her there at the quayside.

The soldiers would travel aboard the QE2. The ocean liner had been acquisitioned by the army to take the troops to the Falkland Islands. They had boarded over all the expensive carpets and secured its valuables safely away. It would have to remain in tip-top shape to supply luxury cruises for those who could afford it after the mission expired. There were rumours that they would feed the soldiers salmon and that they would enjoy the same expensive cuisine that a regular QE2 passenger would have. This was a far cry from the army food of pie and mash that they were used to. For the first time in his career, Jimmy felt worthy of accepting a little luxury and was looking forward to getting the job done and returning home to his beautiful family. This time he would become a good husband and father; thankful that Sheila still loved him enough to give him another chance.

Chapter 5

1996 cont.

Jamie spent a lot of her time with a boy named Ricky Webster. They grew up together on the same street and if there was trouble happening, they were usually in the middle of it. He was a year older and followed her everywhere. Although they talked about everything, he was not the type to have a sympathetic ear, or so she thought. The only time she had tried was when they were sharing a spliff over the quarry. She was looking over to her shed at the bottom of the garden and had told him about a time when her father was hitting her mother. Michael had climbed on his back to try to stop him, so her father locked him in the shed. He was only eleven at the time and was so scared of the dark he pissed himself. Ricky burst into uncontrollable laughter when he heard the story and called her brother a woose.

Jamie was so offended that he would say such a thing. She walked off and didn't see him for a week after that. What she didn't realise was that Ricky had suffered a similar situation at the hands of his older brothers and to laugh about it was his way of dealing with things. They were both hiding from their own demons, but for Jamie that would be the last time, she would look for his softer side. The next time she saw him, he apologised for being so childish. He blamed his actions on the fact that they were stoned and couldn't cope with the severity of it all. She accepted this could have been the case as outbursts of laughter and no concentration came with the game.

Ricky's parents had never earned an honest day's pay in their lives; they had scrounged off the social for every-thing and the rest of their belongings had come from the back of a lorry, no questions asked. His father Tom was a likeable character. He had twinkling Irish eyes and a strong Belfast accent. He was always ready to do a quick fiddle for cash if the price was right. Ricky had a sister and two very violent brothers which all had cars, kids and no jobs. On the plus side, they always brought him cans of beer when they came to visit, and he was never short of foreign fags.

Later that evening Jamie and Ricky went on their usual mooch around the park. She didn't want to drink too much as she knew she needed a clear head to face the next day. Ricky rolled up a spliff and tucking his greasy long hair behind his ears, he looked up at Jamie. 'You're quiet tonight mate—want me to try a few cars—we could down a few cans then bomb around the Red Rec?'

This was his remedy for fixing everything. He may not have been a good listener, but if you had a problem or something was getting you down, he could take you to the brink of your life in an old Ford Escort, taking your mind off everything apart from survival. Jamie accepted his offer of cruising the recreation ground. It was always best to stay out as long as she could when her dad had been drinking, and today was benefit collection day.

As soon as it was dark enough to prowl, they left the park. Both had their hoods up over their heads and pulled down low in the front to cover their faces. They kept their heads down and didn't look up in case there were any neighbourhood watchers around. They made their way to Beechwood Hill in minutes. This was always the best place to steal a car from with the least chance of getting caught as the houses had large sloping front gardens and were a long way from the roadsides. They split up to operate faster, Ricky took the left-hand side of the street and Jamie the right. Whilst wearing their sleeves as gloves, they gave all the door handles a quick try to see if some unexpected victim had left their car door open. This was always the quietest way to play the game. If that didn't work, they would have to smash a window and risk the chance of being heard.

'Bingo,' Ricky whispered as he waved over to Jamie. The car that had chosen him was an old black Ford and easy to hot wire. These were their preferred type as some models you could use a screwdriver to start the engine. It was also the safer option by not having to rip out the steering column and chance getting caught. They took a quick glance around to see if anyone was looking out of their windows, then Ricky convinced Jamie that it was her turn to sort out the streetlight.

'Christ, it's always me. I'm scared of heights mate this is not a good idea.'

'Bollocks, you're a lot smaller than me and can climb a lot faster. Get up there before someone comes to the window.'

Jamie scaled the lamppost in seconds. She had a lot of upper body strength for a teenage girl. She gripped the post with her legs and flipped open the cage. As she tried frantically to unscrew the bulb, she burnt her fingers and had to stop a few times to blow them. She had cut her fingers in the past by smashing the bulb so thought this the less painful option, but now wasn't so sure. She unhooked her legs and slid the rest of the way down the post before hitting the floor with a thud.

They pushed the car halfway down the hill, then jumped in to start the engine with a screwdriver. They were in luck; it worked the first time. As soon as they turned the corner, Jamie began rifling through the cassette tapes to see which ones were worth keeping. After checking each one, she threw them over her shoulder onto the back seat. 'It's all 70s shit mate, there's nothing here for us.'

'Some of that 70s shit is good stuff, Jay, watch what you're chucking out.'

'I don't think you want to remix Val fucking Doonican mate.' She opened the window and threw the cassette out before starting on the glove compartment. As soon as the flap opened, a diary fell into her lap. It was full of bits of loose paper and marked tabs. While she was picking some bits off the floor, she noticed a name she recognised on the top of a letter. 'Rick, you're not going to believe whose car this is.' She flicked through the pages, then read out a statement.

May 12th, Jamie Taylor was seen climbing over the barrier and exiting the school grounds. An older boy that appeared to have been her boyfriend was sat waiting for her arrival on a gold BMX push-bike. They were travelling too fast for me to apprehend them, so a formal letter will be sent from the school board to the girl's parents.

'The Scooby,' shouted Ricky. 'He won't be catching anyone tomorrow Jamie unless he buys a new pair of Nikes.'

They sped down the hill and back towards the park. Ricky mounted the pavement and swerved the car into a concrete post, knocking off a side mirror as he drove the car down a walkway out of sight. 'Oops, sorry Mr School board man, but it had to be done. You don't want to catch your ugly fucking mug in that thing anyway, so I did you a favour.'

With dipped headlights they skidded the car over the field and headed down in second gear towards the lake, keeping just far enough away from the farmhouse windows. A layer of mist carpeted the field as the car dipped in and out of the mud hills. As they drove through the trees and back on to the lane, something sprang out of the bushes in front of them. They both jumped in shock and Jamie started panicking, screaming at Ricky.

Stop! Stop the fucking car mate, you might have hit it!'

Ricky carried on, looking in his rear-view mirror. 'You are joking, right? The first rule in a horror movie: you never get out of the fucking car down a dark lane when something jumps out in front of you.'

'Ricky just stop the fucking car, or I will!' Jamie pulled on the handbrake and swerved the car around. When they stopped being thrown from side to side, they froze, staring into the darkness. 'Look, it's over there in the bushes.'

Jamie got out of the car and started walking towards it, followed by a very reluctant Ricky.

'This is crazy Jamie; I'm going back to the car. Whatever is in there can have you first, I'm off to get a head start.'

Ricky headed back to the car while Jamie went deeper into the bushes. She could hear a rustling sound and followed it to a clearing. It was an animal, but she couldn't quite see what kind. She climbed back out quietly and saw Ricky sitting in the car. He was looking through the Scooby's diary, so he didn't see Jamie hiding by the side of the window, waiting to scare him. She bided her time and as soon as he lifted his head up, she squashed her face up to the glass, peering in at him. He screamed like a girl and climbed across to the passenger seat before realising it was her. Jamie was laughing uncontrollably.

'You were scared shitless.'

'You twat—you were lucky I realised it was you or I would have run you the fuck over.'

As Ricky got out of the car to get back into the driver's side, they heard a rustling behind them. The animal had made its way back on to the road. It looked like a fox with his head stuck in a family size bag of crisps, wandering around blind in the dark.

'Jesus Jay, we can't leave the poor thing like that; we'll have to pull it off.' Ricky broke off a branch and cautiously started poking at the crisp packet while jumping backwards in fear every time the fox moved. Jamie couldn't control herself and fell about laughing.

'This is the funniest thing I have ever seen you do, you're a mad bastard, Ricky Webster.'

He gave a sarcastic smile at Jamie and started poking at the fox again. 'For fuck's sake mate, I'm only trying to help, keep still you little bugger!'

Ricky gave it one last whack of the stick and it was off. The fox looked dazed for a few seconds and blinked from the headlights of the car. He then shook his head, picked up the crisp packet in his mouth and ran back into the trees. Ricky was amazed and turned around to see his friend squatting down.

'I nearly pissed myself mate literally, I just couldn't hold it in, your face was so relieved when you knocked it off—and when he picked it back up, I thought you were going to bash him over the head with the stick.'

'Ha fucking ha Jamie Taylor. Well, at least it put a smile on your face. Let's go home I've had enough drama for one night.'

They drove the car back to Beechwood Hill and left it in the same place as they had found it. Normally they would have set fire to it over the Red Rec, but they had decided that it would be more fun to use it again, another time. They wiped away any fingerprints they might have left and tidied up the inside.

'Shit, Ricky, what about the mirror?'

'Well, I ain't going back to get it, Jay, anyway, he will think that a passing car has knocked it off, don't worry.'

They legged it back home to the estate and took a shortcut through the shops. It was nearly kicking out time at the social club and from the edge of the steel railings, she could see her father with a pint in one hand and a fag in the other staggering around outside. They were far enough away not to be noticed, but she kept her head down just in case.

'He's not gonna recognise you from here Jay, it looks like he can barely stand.'

'I can feel his eyes in the back of my head mate, you can't be too careful, the fucker would throw that glass at me from there if he knew I was out with you, you know what he's like.'

'I'd like to see him try. I'd make him eat the broken glass, the drunken bastard. Let's get you home before he does.'

Chapter 6

The next morning Jamie had purposely put on her tight black jeans. She knew that the teachers would give her a disciplinary for doing so but there was no way she was going to wear a skirt today. She needed to feel more like herself if she were to brave whatever lay ahead of her. Her tie was in a pin knot and she had her brother's boots on—she was happy. After checking herself for one last time in the mirror, she left for school, late as always.

By the time she made it through the gates, registration was over, and the first lesson was about to start. Under normal circumstances, she would have let the fat little school inspector, with his tight pinstripe suit and dirty shoes, mark it down in his little black book as an absence. But not today. Even though she loved to goad him by skipping off to the Red Rec in front of him, she knew that today she had to be allowed into school. She already had a sense of owning him after joyriding in his car the night before, so this time she didn't mind playing by the rules and apologised. She also sincerely apologised to the receptionist on entry and asked to be allowed into class with a late mark. The receptionist was taken aback when Jamie gave her the reason for her lateness and felt sorry for her in a receptionist sort of way. Her dad had vomited all over the bathroom last night, and she had had the pleasure of cleaning it up this morning before she could shower. The stench was unbelievable. He had ripped the shower curtain down by grabbing it to save himself from falling into the bath, of which he often did. Jamie's ceramic frog soap dish she had made in junior school had been smashed to pieces. She had cut her fingers as she picked it out from around the plughole. This hurt her more than she realised and not just from the cuts.

* * *

It was lunchtime before she had a glimpse of Heather. They had no classes together today, but she knew her timetable better than she knew her own, so could find her easy enough. Thursday's, Heather would have had double math's, so she waited for her outside the science block knowing she would pass that way to the canteen.

It wasn't long before Jamie caught sight of her. She watched with intent to the reaction on Heather's face, hoping she would not see in it any regret. Her worries were unfounded. As soon as she saw Jamie waiting for her, a welcoming smile shone from her crescent lips. She whispered something to Abi, and her friend nodded and walked on in front.

'Hey you,' she smiled. Jamie's stomach jerked. Even the sound of her voice was enough to have a reaction.

She looked excitedly into her shiny green eyes. She wanted to kiss her there and then, but controlled her wanting. 'I thought I'd wait for you—was that OK? I didn't know if you'd wanna see me or not, what with it being school and all.'

'Are you mad—I've thought of nothing else all morning. Shall we see if we can find somewhere quiet to chat? I've got some lunch in my bag that we can share.'

They nervously headed for the playing field behind the science block and sat on the bank out of view. Heather opened her bag to reveal some neatly wrapped ham sandwiches and offered one to Jamie. 'No thanks,' Jamie replied as she lay leaning with her head on her hand while her elbow nestled in the fresh-cut grass. Food was the last thing on her mind right now as her stomach felt as if a tsunami was brewing from inside.

'I saw you last night on the bridge from my dad's car. He drove me home after netball practice. I did wave, but I guess you didn't see me—you were with someone. Is that your boyfriend, then?' Heather asked inquisitively.

Jamie laughed. 'Christ no, that's Ricky, he's just a mate.' Heather felt embarrassed and wished that she had kept her assumptions to herself.

'I just wondered, as I've seen you with him a couple of times now.'

Now who's the stalker, Jamie thought. 'Yeah, we spend a lot of time together, but it's nothing like that. Not like you and that geek Dexter you're seeing. You two act like an old married couple.'

'Marriage, God, that would never happen. We've been seeing each other since primary school, but Dex is more like an annoying friend than anything else. Most of the time I can't stand him.'

'I bet he doesn't think that' Jamie implied, knowing that if she were in his shoes, friendship would be the last thing on her mind.

'No, you're right, he's been hassling me a lot lately to—you know,' she frowned and felt even more embarrassed.

'Know what?' Jamie smirked just to wind her up.

'Stop teasing me Jamie, you know exactly what I mean.' Heather pushed Jamie's shoulder, and she fell back on to the grass laughing.

'It's not funny—I have a hard-enough time kissing him lately without his hands crawling all over me,' she shuddered physically. 'It's like—I know I should want him to, and he's a really good-looking guy, but I just can't go through with it—something doesn't feel right.'

Jamie stayed quiet and watched Heather pack away her lunchbox, as she continued,

'Most of my friends have slept with their boyfriends, but I don't think I'm ready for all that. Then when I felt I had feelings for you I got even more confused.'

Jamie stared at her for a little while, then started giggling. 'Sorry, I shouldn't laugh it was just the way your face looked, it went all red and blushy like. I'm sure it must be hard for you. So why don't you just finish with him?'

'I want to, but I don't know how to without my mum and dad asking questions. They are good friends with his parents. We even went on holiday together last year to the Algarve. That was a joke he spent half the time trying to whisk me off to these quiet little nooks on the beach and the other half lying in bed with a sick stomach and his mummy looking after him.' She rolled her eyes. 'That was all his fault, trying to be macho and eat all the local dishes. He didn't have a clue what they were but made out he'd eaten them hundreds of times.'

Jamie remembered her holiday last year, camping in Rhyl with the youth club. She had accidentally on purpose climbed into Julie Smith's sleeping bag. She knew that she was up for it as they had enjoyed a quick fumble in a cupboard earlier that day. The fact that the youth leaders had caught them in the throes of young passion didn't help matters much, though. She didn't know who was the most embarrassed, them or her and Julie. Because of their antics, they cut the camping trip short, and she never saw Julie again.

'I am still trying to break it off, but he just can't take the hint,' Heather explained.

'I told him I wanted to concentrate on my exams and couldn't go out with him after school anymore, but he kept making excuses. He had the cheek to ask my parents if he could come over to the house to study. That made things a lot worse as we were spending even more time alone. My mum and dad adore him, they already have visions of us married with kids—he's turned into a bit of a creep, a right little parent pleaser.'

Jamie listened to Heather's predicament and thought about how she could help. She would just tell him straight to piss off, but somehow, she didn't think Heather could be as blunt. 'I think your gonna have to be honest with him and tell him you're not interested or it's only gonna get worse.'

'Yeah, you're right, either that or tell him to PISS OFF,' Heather scowled.

Jamie laughed, maybe she could be that blunt she thought. 'So, what are you up to tonight, do you want to do something–or are you studying with Dexter?'

'Ha-ha, hilarious. You can walk me home from school if you like—that is, if you can stand walking by the side of me instead of stalking me from behind.'

'I think I can handle that.'

* * *

Two weeks had passed, and Jamie knew that she was falling hard for her girl. The time they had spent together after school every day had brought them closer together. After a few white lies on both sides, they had even managed a trip to the cinema and as far as the world was concerned, they were typical school friends, just out for laughs. They were getting good at keeping their private life a secret, at lesson times they made sure to keep their distance as much as they could bear so as not to draw attention to their friendship. They always spent lunchtimes at the canal or behind the science block, far enough for people not to notice them.

Morning classes had been stressful. The teachers had received news of someone selling cannabis in the locker room, and a search was being made for the culprit. At lunchtime, they were glad to be away from it all. Their trip to the grass bank behind the science block had seemed miles away from all the pushing and shoving of kids trying to hide stuff from the teachers' searching eyes. They would just laze there together and make plans for the weekend. They were comfortable as a couple now and hated it when they had to leave each other. Jamie looked unwillingly at her watch, then leaned over to Heather and stole a kiss. She knew it was risky, but the need was too compelling. Heather felt the intense longing too and responded by putting her hand around Jamie's neck, pulling her towards her. The kiss started soft and subtle, but the more they enjoyed each other, the more reckless it became. Lost in a deep embrace, the reality of them being in school held no bearing on their actions. Heather sighed as Jamie's hand lowered towards her waist, pulling their bodies tighter together. She was almost on top of her as their emotions were drawing them closer to forbidden contact. The unwanted screech from the school siren caused them to pull away frantically as it jolted them back to the present. They were now fully aware that they had left themselves open to prying eyes. In haste, they grabbed their things together, scrambled to their feet and ran anxiously across the field to their separate destinations.

Feeling pumped full of adrenalin, Jamie wasn't in the mood for school anymore. She couldn't stop thinking of Heather and felt that if she didn't leave now, she wouldn't be able to control herself. She climbed the back fence and ran most of the way home. Heather had promised to meet up with her in the park later that evening, and Jamie was already dreaming of what the night would bring. She knew that her mother wouldn't mind if she skipped school, as she would be glad of the company. She had often asked Jamie to stay home, especially if she had had a bad time the night before.

When Jamie arrived home, she found her mother Sheila sat at the kitchen table hugging a cold cup of cof-

fee and staring obliviously into space. She lit up a fag
and gave it to her mother, then lit one for herself.

'Are you OK, Mam?'

Sheila flinched in pain as Jamie put her arm around
her. She had harboured thoughts about killing her father
for the way he treated her mother. It frustrated her that
her mother always blamed herself and stood by him, no
matter how evil he was. It was as if her mother felt like
she deserved all the beatings and the cruelty that she
had to face every day.

'I'm OK love, your dad had a bad day, that's all.'

'Why don't you ask Auntie Sal if you can stay with
her for a couple of days, you look terrible?

Jamie knew that her words were wasted. Her father
hated Sal for grassing him up to Sheila's parents about
the beatings, so she wasn't allowed to talk to her on the
phone let alone visit. Sal had also threatened him with
getting the boys from the pub to 'duff him up' so she was
staying well clear.

His time in the Falklands had changed her dad's personality completely. They discharged him from the army
on medical grounds, and he wasn't the same man when
he returned home. The constant sweat-filled nightmares
gave him no peace. When awake, the flashbacks clawed
at his sanity making it hard to hold down a job because
of his violent outbursts of temper. Sheila had vowed to
stand by *her* Jimmy as she called him, and that's what
she did no matter what. The war had created more than
one casualty for the family. Sheila could never forgive

herself for the wrongdoing that took place around that time. It gave her a guilty secret that she kept hidden from the outside world. It was the reason she took the beatings with no retaliation, and it ate her up more and more every day. Even though the jealousy from his mistakes brought her to the brink of no return, she never used this as an excuse for her unlawful behaviour in a moment of madness. Not knowing whether the 'mistake' or her husband, was her son Michael's father, plagued her. She battled continually with the prospect, harbouring the guilt-ridden secret, of which she shared with no one.

'What's the time, love? Your dad will be home for his tea soon.'

'It's OK Mam you've got ages yet, I came home from school early today.'

Shelia held her face in her hands, then tucked her lank, lifeless hair behind her ears. 'That's nice love, make yourself useful and cut some chips for your dad and Mikey, will you? It'll save me doing it later.'

Jamie hacked out the bad bits from some rubbery old potatoes and left them soaking in water.

'Thanks, babe. You'll make someone a good wife one day love, I don't know what I'd do without you.' Sheila said humbly.

Jamie had been doing housework from a very early age. Where the other kids were being taught the dangers of touching an iron she had been figuring out how to use one, she didn't mind and enjoyed helping her mother out. When she was little, her mother used to have her bringing her cups of tea in bed, before she got up in the morning. She would try her hardest not to spill any on the journey to the top of the stairs but always managed to tip some right outside the bedroom door while taking her eye off the cup to push down the handle. A build-up of drips had made the carpet crunch underfoot from the years of sugary tea spills engraved into the weave. This didn't deter Jamie. She would stand there and wait patiently for her mother to sip it and tell her it was the best tea she had ever tasted; this would always put a smile on her face.

Later that afternoon, Michael came home from school. As he pushed passed Jamie to climb the stairs, she noticed that his face had been battered and bruised. He had tried to hide it from her, but she had caught sight of him in the hallway mirror.

Her dad had always hit her mother on the body well out of the sight of do-gooders and awkward questions. He had given Jamie and Michael the odd punch, kick and thrash with his belt but nothing as bad as this. The shock fuelled her anger even more. How did he think he would get away with this? The boy was only fourteen years old, for Christ's sake. Someone would ask questions for sure.

Jamie crept up the stairs and stood listening through Michael's door. She could hear him sobbing and swallowed hard, trying to contain her own tears before tapping gently.

'Mikey open up, Bro.'

'Fuck off and leave me alone! I'm OK.'

She waited for him to change his mind and he could sense her still outside.

'Just fuck off, I don't wanna talk about it!'

The embarrassment had obviously taken hold of him, she thought. He had always been petrified of his father, and he knew when to keep his head down and say nothing.

'OK mate, but I'm here if you need me.'

The silence was the stern reply. There was nothing she could do about it anyway, she thought. Unless her mother went to the police it would always be her dad's word against theirs, and he always got his own way. Jamie respected her brother's wishes and went back to her own room to get ready for her date with Heather.

Chapter 7

The park was empty when she arrived. It was too late for the younger ones to have been daring each other to ride the killer cradle and too early for the teenagers to get their kicks from sharing a bottle of vodka under the climbing frame. Jamie perched on the swing and waited patiently for Heather. It felt surreal to be there sober, Jamie thought. Normally by now she was on her third can of Special and had had a few spliffs under her belt.

Heather's family lived just outside the estate in a large private house and always seemed so normal compared to the crazies she lived with. Their backgrounds couldn't be more different yet still, she had to pursue this. Even if it meant her hiding her own dysfunctional family life, it would be worth it to act as a regular teenager for a change.

At home, she took on the roles of a housewife and mother to Michael when he needed a bit of TLC. She wasn't that much older but did her best and always looked out for him, even when they were small.

At primary school, he would run to her crying if someone had picked on him. She would storm around the playground, find the culprit, and give them a black eye to make sure they knew who they were dealing with. When her father found out, he would give her a slap for getting involved and not letting him fight his own battles. Now they were older. He didn't rely on her so much for protection, but she kept a close eye on him even still. Her mother was on so many tablets for depression that she was a walking zombie most of the time. Jamie had felt the most responsible out of all the Taylor family, even with her own troubles brewing in the background.

Two hours had passed and still no sign of Heather. She was feeling a bit of a fool for waiting so long and hoped that there would be a good explanation for her not turning up. She lit up a fag for courage and began the walk down the hill to Heather's house for the first time.

Jamie hadn't planned to knock on the door, but as she arrived, she found Heather looking attentively out of her window. As soon as she saw Jamie, she signalled for her to come closer. She opened the door just as Jamie took her last step, then pulling her jumper around her shoulders she stepped out. Still holding the door open an inch, she shouted back at her dad.

'I'm popping out for a minute I won't be long.'

Not waiting for a reply, she hurried Jamie away from the front door and led her to another large building at the back of the house. Her hand was shaking as she forced the key into the door, before practically pushing Jamie through it.

Inside, framed college certificates adorned the walls with rows of box files standing neatly in cabinets. Huge black leather sofas gave it a warm and inviting feeling, but not for her, she surmised. Jamie's entire house could have fitted inside the building that they were using as a study, and it made Jamie totally aware of how different these girls' backgrounds really were.

'Heather, it's OK, I get the hint you don't want your parents seeing me—don't worry, I'll go.'

'Oh my god, Jamie, if only it was that easy. It's got nothing to do with my parents. I can't believe you took the risk of coming around here after what happened to Michael today. I hoped that you'd have had more sense to leave it for a while.' Heather's voice screamed desperation as Jamie's confusion developed.

She quickly dropped the window blinds and locked the door before pulling Jamie towards her. 'It's not safe for either of us to be seen together. What if those maniacs that jumped your brother had seen you coming here?'

Jamie couldn't believe what she was hearing she was so quick to assume that it was her father's handy work she had never dreamed that there could have been anyone else involved. 'What are you talking about—who jumped Michael? I don't understand. What's it got to do with us?'

Heather looked bewildered she couldn't believe that Jamie knew nothing of today's events. 'Jamie, it's got everything to do with us. We were the reason he suffered such a beating.'

She could see Michael's battered little face in her head when she closed her eyes. She would make somebody pay for this big time. Heather was still shaking as she tried to get the rest of the story out in between her deep breaths.

'That scrawny little runt Martin saw us on the field at lunchtime. He was probably up to something dodgy as usual or hiding from someone, anyway, he came back to school shouting his mouth off about you and some girl rolling around on the field together and as you can imagine he added a lot more detail to the story. Luckily, he didn't get a good enough look at me or I think I would have ended up in the same state as Michael.'

Jamie could feel her palms filling with sweat, so she nervously rubbed them down the legs of her jeans and sat on the edge of the black leather sofa that almost filled the wall.

'I'm so sorry, Heather. I would never have come here if I'd known.'

Jamie suddenly remembered who Martin was, and fear shot through her body.

'Is this the Martin that hangs around with the Thompson boys?' Jamie asked while jumping to her feet.

'Yes—unfortunately. We are in big trouble, Jamie.'

The Thompson boys were known around the estate for their lack of toleration to any of the minorities. They were racist thugs but hated queers most of all. Last year they had terrorised a family of a boy who took dancing lessons. He wasn't even gay, but that made no difference to them. Dancing was for poofs, so he must be one. Rumour had it they had tied him to a tree and covered him in spray paint with the words faggot and bum boy all over his naked body. An old lady who had been out walking her dog eventually found him and called the police. As usual, nothing happened as the boy wouldn't give out any names for the fear of repercussions.

This was how things worked around the estate: you wouldn't grass anyone up to the police unless you had an army of people behind you. Even then you would have to be sure that the army was completely on your side.

Heather headed back towards the door. 'I won't be too long. I just need to tell my dad I'm out here, so he doesn't come looking for me. Would you like a coke or something?'

'Have you got any vodka? I don't think that coke will hit the spot.'

She smiled, but still, the panic showed visibly on her face as she turned and left.

After pacing around, Jamie sat back down, trying to make sense of what was happening. If they went for Michael, they would surely hatch some plan for her.

Heather returned with the coke, and a bottle of her father's whiskey hidden under her jumper.

'Will this do you?' she said while waving the bottle in front of her. 'My dad always keeps a bottle in the kitchen cupboard in case we have any guests. He hardly ever drinks, and yet clients insist on buying him whiskey to say thank you for cooking their books for them. I told him I'm down here studying so we won't be disturbed.' She turned the key in the lock once more, just in case.

Jamie had liked the words won't be disturbed and felt guilty of her thoughts. Michael had taken such a beating because of her, and yet the realisation that she was now alone with Heather was slowly creeping to the forefront of her mind.

Jamie took a swig from the whisky bottle, then handed it to Heather. She took it from her, then took two glasses out of the cabinet to fill.

'Do you want me to leave?' Jamie whispered, not really wanting a reply.

'No—no way. Then the bullies would have won. I can't believe that they get away with treating people like this. We just have to be more careful that's all and try to come up with a way of sorting things out.' Heather sat herself down on the sofa next to Jamie. Even though the initial instinct for Heather was to panic, Jamie could see a lot of fighting spirit in her too.

'You're beautiful when you're angry. Do you know that?' Jamie leaned over and looked deep into Heather's terrified eyes. 'We'll think of something, I know we will. I wouldn't let you get hurt, and that's a promise.'

She could feel Jamie's cool whiskey-breath on her face as she moved in for a kiss. The sheer desperation was immediately reciprocated. All of today's events seemed to control their actions, fuelling their need for one another. Wrapping their bodies around each other with a mix of anger and lust, they fell to the floor. Both girls' inhibitions were stripped bare. They needed a release from the pent-up aggression that dwelled within.

As Heather straddled Jamie, she lifted her arms to pull her jumper up over her head. Then throwing her hair to one side, she started kissing her neck. 'Don't stop. I want you to.'

She bit her lip and closed her eyes as she felt Jamie loosening her jeans. Her body lifted as Jamie flicked open her button. Heather held on tight around Jamie's neck, and with each movement, she breathed a deep sigh of pleasure. She had lost all feeling in both of her legs, and this made it unbearable for Heather not to lose complete control. Lifting her hips one last time, she made it obvious to Jamie that she wanted for her to release the pressure that she had created.

Heather's face blushed at the thought of what had happened between them and at first, could not look Jamie in the eye. She paused to catch her breath. Not wanting to let go of her, but also too embarrassed to stay, Heather nervously rose to her feet. As the feelings in her legs were only just beginning to come back, she buckled faintly before attempting to get dressed, then after straightening herself out, she nervously poured them another drink.

'I hope you don't think I make a habit of this—I'm really not like that at all. I don't know what came over me. It's not like I'm easy or anything.'

'Heather, I would never think of you like that. You're amazing and I'm way out of my league being with you.'

Too shy and self-conscious to talk about her actions anymore, she suggested to Jamie that she should leave now while it was still light. Jamie understood and was feeling a bit overwhelmed herself.

The walk home unnerved her. Although she was still smiling inside at the thought of her encounter with Heather, she had a lot of trouble to sort out and explaining things to Michael would be no simple task. What would she say to him? And had he told her parents? Her father would go ballistic if he knew that everyone was talking about them.

As she walked out from the tunnel, the same tunnel that they had shared their first kiss, she felt something hit the back of her leg, and then her head, she turned to see Wayne and Kevin Thompson standing on top of the bridge, tossing stones in their hands.

The oldest boy Wayne was twenty now, despite that, anyone smaller than him was still an open target. They both lived at home with their domineering mother and she gave them all the alibis they would ever need, topped off with the odd slap and plenty of verbal abuse.

'Oi Dyke where d'ya think you're going?'

They hurled another larger stone at her from above, which luckily, she dodged. Too scared to answer, she ran as fast as she could towards the park. Behind her, she could hear each thumping footstep getting closer.

'There's no point running. We know where you live, don't forget.'

The constant running had given her a stitch in her side, which made it almost impossible to carry on. She held onto it tight to ease the pain before eventually reaching the park. It was still dead and sat on the swing was Wayne Thompson waiting for her. As she turned to run back into the bushes to escape, she ran straight into Kevin Thompson. The two brothers dragged her back into the bushes and out of sight from the park.

'Get off me or I swear you'll regret it. My old man will come looking for you.'

She struggled aimlessly as the younger of the boys tackled her to the floor. She managed to roll herself onto her front and crawl her way through the dirt. Desperately looking around, she found half a brick which she held close to her chest. As the boy started dragging her back by her legs, she twisted her body around and whacked him across the face with it. His mouth spurted out blood and then a tooth to follow. Jamie scrambled to her feet as quick as her legs would let her.

Blood dribbled from the boy's mouth, and he wiped it across his sleeve. 'Look what that fucker has done to me!'

The older brother, furious that she had fought back, punched Jamie clean in the face and knocked her flat back onto the ground. 'You're gonna pay for this, Taylor. You wanna fuck women, do you? I'll show you how you fuck women,' he smiled over to his brother. 'Kev rip her shirt open and pin her down, I'm going to enjoy this.'

The youngest of the brothers climbed on top and forced her hands to the floor while the older brother Wayne started undoing his jeans. Tugging at his studded belt, he pulled it through the loops then cracked it like a whip across her naked chest. She screamed out in agony. Luckily for her, the scream and the boy's sick laughter didn't go unheard as Ricky appeared out of nowhere holding a crowbar.

'Oi Thompson, get your fucking hands off my girlfriend before I get my brothers down here to batter the fuck out of you.'

'She's not your girlfriend Webster; she's a dirty little dyke. The lezza was shagging some girl on the school field earlier, Martin saw them, now fuck off and mind your own business.'

'Martin is a lying tosser. It was me she was with at lunchtime. I know I've got long hair but I ain't a fucking girl, am I? That stoner wouldn't recognise his own reflection in a mirror when he's smoking that shit. I should know, I fucking sold it to him. Now fuck off and leave her alone.'

Wayne Thompson did up his jeans and backed away. He took one last look at Jamie lying bruised and exposed on the floor, then spat in her face. 'You're lucky this time Taylor but if you dare open your mouth about this to anyone, we'll be back to finish the job, your brothers don't scare me, Webster, I just wasn't in the mood to fuck a dyke today. But I will be next time.'

Ricky helped Jamie to her feet as the brothers went off to hound some other poor unexpected victim.

'Who's been a naughty girl then?' he said sarcastically.

'Shut the fuck up and help me stand.' As Jamie stood and took her balance, blood was seeping out of the stud marks on her chest.

'That *was* a lucky escape, Jay. What if I hadn't been here to save your arse?'

Sick welled up in her mouth as she imagined what might have happened. She spat it out on to the floor with a shudder. 'I would have sorted it, they're just wankers,' she started brushing herself down. Under her breath, Jamie knew that she wouldn't have been able to sort it and thanked God that Ricky had turned up when he did, but she wasn't ready to admit defeat just yet.

'So, who was it you were shagging on the field then? And you could have told me you were a fucking dyke it would have given me something to think about, late at night if you get what I mean.' He suggested to her a hand movement which also turned her stomach.

'You are a fucking wanker Ricky, do you know that? It's not something you just come out with, mate; I was having a bad enough time coming to terms with it myself without you taking the piss out of me.' She struggled to pull her shirt back together.

'Yeah, I know, I know. Are you OK?'

'Yeah, just fucking peachy mate. Look at the state of me!' As she looked down at herself, she could see that her blood had soaked through her shirt. 'What the fuck am I gonna do now?' She winced at the pain and a single tear tracked down her dirty face.

Secretly Ricky couldn't bear to see her like this, so he tried to take the edge off the situation in his own way. 'You're gonna have a few cans with me, then I'll take you home to mine and we'll get you cleaned up, so you don't get stupid questions off that crazy arse father of yours.'

He cracked open a can of Special and handed it to Jamie.

'Cheers mate, sorry it's just this is nasty shit, y'know. Wait till you see what they did to Michael.'

'I've seen him. He told me what happened, that's why I came looking for you. You're gonna have to speak to him mate he fucking hates you at the moment.'

Jamie already knew that would be the case. Michael was fucked up in the head enough without this towering over him, she thought.

'I know, I'll talk to him about it. So, what about you—do you hate me too?'

Ricky put his arm around his mate's shoulders. 'Yeah—but I always thought you were a twat, so my opinion doesn't mean Jack.'

They finished the pack of four cans and Ricky helped Jamie back to his house.

As they reached their street, she noticed that her house was in darkness apart from the one bare bulb in Michael's room shining through the curtains that didn't quite meet in the middle.

They went into Ricky's house via the back door and he sat Jamie down at the kitchen table before he went upstairs.

Ricky's house was exactly the same as Jamie's only facing the other way around. They were all tightly knitted together in a row at the edge of the estate. Not long after, his mother came into the kitchen in her winceyette dressing gown. She was so startled to see Jamie sitting there that the unlit fag that was hanging from her lip fell to the floor.

'What the hell happened to you, kid? I hope you gave as good as you got—Oh my god, where's Ricky is he OK?'

'Yeah, he's fine, I just had a bit of an accident, that's all.'

'I'm not asking any questions love it's your business, I keep out of things me love as you well know, but if you need anything just come and get me, OK.'

Ricky returned and gave an acknowledged nod to his mother as he ushered Jamie up the stairs to the bathroom.

'Here are some towels and shit—and one of my T-shirts, it should be OK.'

'Thanks, mate I'll be out of here as soon as I look a bit normal.'

'That would take forever. I haven't got all night Taylor just get in there and tidy yourself up,' he said with a smirk. 'We'll try to sneak you across the road into your house out of harm's way before your dad gets home from the pub.'

Chapter 8

Next morning Jamie winced as she opened her eyes. She tried to move, but the bedsheet was stuck to her chest with thick dried blood. After painfully peeling it away from her still quite open wounds, she carefully crawled out of bed. She bundled the sheet together and hid it at the bottom of her wardrobe underneath the clothes that no longer fitted her before taking a shower.

Her body stung like an attack of bees when the water pounded against her bare flesh. Her tears were hidden well under the droplets that were falling off her face as the steaming hot water cleaned her open wounds. She chose a dark towel to wrap herself in before rifling through the cupboards, searching for protection. A wad of clean cotton wool would have to do. She quickly tip-toed across the landing, her hair sopping the carpet as she hurriedly made it back to the safety of her room. With a few rounds of sticky tape, she managed to keep the wad in place and hoped it would last through the day.

Yesterday was a close call, but she had Ricky's version of events to fall back on, so any comments that were aimed at her in school today she could deal with. The incident with the Thompson brothers sat vivid in her mind and although she dared to think of what might have happened if Ricky hadn't turned up, she knew that she was still not out of the water completely as the threat of their return was pending.

It was still quite early, and she really wanted to see Heather before school, so she threw on the rest of her clothes, a baseball cap, and headed out the door.

After taking the same path that Heather would have taken to school, her intuition paid off, and she caught up with her. Hoping that Heather wouldn't notice the makeshift bandage through her shirt, Jamie pretended as if nothing had happened and startled her from behind.

'Boo.'

Heather jumped in fear. She dropped the books she had been carrying and swung her schoolbag around with full force at her assailant. Even though her face showed a sigh of relief when she saw Jamie standing there, she still wanted to whack her for her precarious actions.

'You scared me half to death, I thought you were one of the Thompson boys!' her emotions overtook her, and tears welled up in her eyes.

Jamie reached out to hold her, regretting instantly the reckless decision of jumping out. 'Heather—calm down—it's OK, it's all been sorted.' Jamie held her as tight as the pain in her chest would let her before Heather pushed her away.

'I nearly peed my pants, you idiot! What were you thinking?'

'I know I'm sorry, but it's OK now, honestly.'

The frightened look on Heather's face had turned to bewilderment as she desperately waited for Jamie's explanation.

'Ricky spoke to the Thompson brothers last night and told them it was him I was with on the field, not a girl, and the stupid thick bastards fell for it.'

'Jamie, he looks nothing like me. They are not that stupid, surely?'

'They must be, they believed it. Ricky has long hair, so he convinced them that Martin was mistaken. They know as well as anyone else that he's the biggest stoner in the school, so now it'll be his word against Martins. We're in the clear Heather, honest.'

Jamie's words consoled her, and you could see the worry drop from her face.

'I couldn't sleep at all last night every sound outside had me looking out the window fearing the worst. Are you sure it's all over?'

'Well, it will be by the end of school today you know how fast rumours spread around that place. We'll be yesterday's news before you know it.'

As they walked back towards Heather's house so she could re-do her makeup before school, they made plans on how to keep a low profile. They had had a lucky escape this time and didn't need any assumptions being made by the gossip brigade. As they got closer, they saw the outline of Jamie's nemesis Dexter, Heather's still boyfriend, coming down the path from her house.

'That's all I need,' she whispered quickly to Jamie, who was already scowling at the sight of him. With his neatly parted hair and a crease in his trousers that you could cut bread with, he sauntered towards her.

'Hey babe, I thought I'd surprise you and walk you to school today.'

He gave an uninviting stare at Jamie, then grabbed Heather's arm as he turned his back.

'What are you doing talking to that! Didn't you hear what happened in school yesterday?' He whispered in Heather's ear but made it obvious he wanted Jamie to overhear everything. 'She was seen kissing some girl on the field—she's a lesbian Heather you want to be careful with people like that, she'll be after you next.' He tried to take Heather with him as he walked away, but she shrugged off his hold.

'Let go of me. What are you doing here, anyway? Do I have to spell it out for you we said we were going to have a break for a while so quit following me around everywhere?'

Feeling humiliated at being talked down to by Heather, Dexter started to get rattled and stormed towards them.

'So, is that why you don't want to see me anymore then?' He looked Jamie up and down as he pointed his freshly manicured finger at her. 'It all makes sense now. You'll be shaving your hair off and wearing Dr Martin boots next. Wait till I tell your mum and dad you're a lemon. They are going to go mental.'

Jamie had held her tongue for long enough. She grabbed Dexter by his blazer lapels and put her face as close to his as she possibly could without touching it.

'Why don't you be a nice little boy—and run to the teacher to get your books marked before I mark them for you, you fucking weasel.'

Jamie gave him a soft sarcastic slap across his already embarrassed face and then Dexter pulled away. Shocked at Jamie's actions, he backed off, almost tripping over his feet as he did.

'This is your last chance Heather, I mean it—I'll tell your parents, they have a right to know who you're spending your time with and they won't be very happy that its estate scum like that. Come to school with me now and we'll forget all about it.'

It only took the two steps forward from Jamie to have Dexter running away like the wimpy rich-kid he was. She had forgotten all about the pain in her chest and just wanted to run after him and grapple him to the floor. She couldn't hide her annoyance from Heather and questioned what this would mean to their relationship.

'So, what's the plan now then Heather do you want me to go as well, now your little boyfriend as outed you?'

The tone of her assumptions shocked Heather.

'How dare you? I'm nothing like him, I don't care what people think about me,' she began to walk away then turned on a thought 'I do on the other hand have a fear of what the Thompson brothers are capable of. Dexter will be shouting his mouth off now to anyone who will listen.'

Jamie knew only too well of what they were capable of and had the scars to prove it. But she would keep it a secret for as long as she could. Heather didn't need the worry, and she was big enough to carry that burden on her own back.

'Look, Heather, I'm sorry. I shouldn't have spoken to you like that. It's my fault. I guess I'm not used to trusting people, that's all.'

Heather couldn't help but forgive her She could see in her eyes how much Dexter being around was confusing for her, but she knew only too well how childish he could be when it came to the humiliation of someone he didn't like. They quickly made their way to school. No time now for Heather to go back inside as their altercation with Dexter had made them late enough.

The morning's first two periods dragged as Jamie waited with anticipation of double French with Heather. She heard a couple of loose comments and whispers behind her back but had played along with Ricky's story just to be safe. If anyone got too close to the truth, it

JAMIE'S STORY ~ 99

would be bait for the Thompson boys, and that was the last thing she needed.

As Heather walked into the classroom, all eyes were on her as usual, and as Jamie looked up from her desk, she had no misconceptions that Heather would sit anywhere near her, but she was wrong. Instead of sitting at the front of the class like she usually did, she sat with her friend Abi directly behind Jamie.

As the lesson proceeded, she could hear the odd snigger coming from the two girls behind and had suffered several taps on her shoulder from Heather's ruler. Judging by the way Abi was playing along, it was obvious that Heather had confided in her best friend about the two of them and she didn't seem to have a problem with it. Jamie had her own ideas about Abi and always thought that she might bat for both sides herself. She was a bit of a rock chick with her punky hair and black lipstick and always acted a lot older than she was.

Halfway through the lesson, Duane Wright, a spotty, well-dressed boy in his Clarke's squeaky shoes, had a pop at Jamie through the teacher Miss Halliwell. Thinking he'd be clever he shouted his question with his hand over his face sniggering.

'Miss, what's French for Lesbian?'

The entire class turned to look at Jamie. The comment created a wave of mumbling across the classroom, to the regret of Miss Halliwell.

Abi looked at her friend's embarrassed face and did something completely out of character; she stood up in front of the restless crowd and retaliated.

'Hey zit-face, maybe you should ask your mother—I'm sure she knows.'

She sat back down and slumped in her chair as if nothing had happened. The class roared with laughter. Even Miss Halliwell had a smirked expression as all eyes were on the posh-boy. The comment had caught him by surprise and he had no comeback ready so he hid his spotty red face in his sleeve. Jamie knew of his mother and she was a very trouser wearing woman with a hard mouth so maybe the comment had hit a sore spot that was a bit too close to home, she thought. She laughed along with the rest of them and was glad that her turn for humiliation was over.

Everyone got to their feet and collected their bags. They drowned out the end of lesson bell by the screeching of chair legs across the polished floor. As Jamie slung on her jacket, Miss Halliwell called her to the front of the class. She rolled her eyes, as she automatically thought she was in for detention or something of the same; that was the only time a teacher ever called her to the front of the class for a chat.

She was a smart young woman, always wearing the latest fashion and very attractive. Jamie had harboured a secret crush on her from her first day at school, so was a little apprehensive about talking to her in private. She sat on the edge of her desk and gave Jamie an understanding glance whilst patting the desk for her to sit next to her.

'Jamie, I know school hasn't always been kind to you, but if you ever need to talk about anything, I'm a good listener.'

'It's OK Miss, I'm not worried about idiots like Duane, no brain. They haven't got a clue what they're talking about.'

Jamie revelled in the attention she was getting from her favourite teacher. She could feel the hairs standing up on the back of her neck, so she rubbed it to stop the sensation.

'As long as you're OK.' Jamie could see that she looked a little embarrassed as she started straightening out her flowing skirt that was draping the table. But she kept on talking just the same. 'Unfortunately, rumours have a way of spreading to the staffroom, so I have a good idea of what went on yesterday, I hope you're dealing with things and the others are not giving you too much of a hard time?'

Jamie felt like coming clean there and then as it would have been good to have had some adult advice for a change, but she stayed quiet, she couldn't risk anyone else finding out the truth so kept her head down and didn't comment.

'Well, you know where I am if you need me.'

Jamie nodded, then watched intently as the teacher grabbed her things together to leave. Her perfume always stayed in the class way after she did, and Jamie had often stayed that extra bit longer to be in awe of it. She followed her out reluctantly and instantly regretted that she hadn't opened up to her.

Outside, Heather and Abi were waiting for her in the corridor. As she walked towards them, she could hear them gloating about Abi's comment to Duane.

'That was so funny did you see him shrink back in his seat. I'm on a roll now girls anyone hassle you today and they'll have me to answer to.'

She walked on in front after winking at Heather just to let the girls have a few minutes to themselves.

'I hope you didn't mind me telling Abi, she's a really good friend to me.'

Jamie shook her head and went to talk, but Heather interrupted.

'When I told her, she loved the idea. She thinks your stunning and knows how to keep a secret.'

Heather was sounding more like her old self now, oozing with self-confidence and a smile that would melt an ice cap.

'She wants me to sleep over her house with her tonight as it's Friday and no school tomorrow. She lives with her Gran and she's away this weekend.'

Before Heather could continue, Jamie was already plotting a visit.

'She said you could come over too—if you think your parents will let you.'

Jamie smiled from within. She wanted to burst with an appreciation of Abi's Gran but kept her cool as to not sound too overly ecstatic when accepting. Jamie knew her parents wouldn't mind her going, as she wasn't planning on telling them, but Heather didn't need to know that, and it would be easy to sneak out.

The end of the day couldn't come too soon, Jamie knew that she would have to at least try to smooth things over with Michael. She wanted to start the weekend with a clean slate, worrying about what he would be thinking had made her tense and restless. She had tried all his usual hangout places in school but couldn't find him anywhere. He bunked off as much as she did, so there was no reason to worry or expect anything.

As she passed the ice-cream van on the corner of the school gates, she saw Ricky bumming a fag off a kid from their street. He was on his push-bike and waiting to give her a backy on the way home. He often did this but thought that this time he would make sure that everyone had seen him meeting his so-called girlfriend by making a nuisance of himself around the kids in the queue.

As she held on tight around Ricky's waist, she could feel her wounds seeping with every bump that challenged the bike. The weaving in and out of the traffic made her feel sick, and she felt faint. She was more than glad to get off when they rode into their street.

'Thanks again for last night, Rick. I wouldn't be standing here if it weren't for you. Those bastards would surely have ripped me apart if you hadn't stepped in and lied for me. I'll always remember that mate.'

Ricky gave an acknowledging nod and checked out the tyre on the front of his bike.

'You've covered for my arse loads of times in the past Taylor it's about time I did something for you.'

Jamie smiled, she had a good friend in Ricky even though he was a little rough at the edges. He pulled out a spliff from his top pocket and sat on the kerb.

'Did you hear what Kevin Thompson is saying as to how he got his face smashed in?'

Jamie sat on the kerb next to him and took out her lighter. 'He's telling everyone that it happened in a fight at JoJo's nightclub. As if that scruffy no mark could ever get in there.' She held her hand around the tiny flame. The lighter was low on gas and it took ages to ignite. 'The bouncers would take one look at him and fall about laughing. It's good though, as I don't think he'll be bothering with you again—just in case you tell people that it was you that smashed his face in. He's such a wanker.' Ricky offered the spliff to Jamie, and she took a hard drag as he continued. 'It would ruin him if people knew that a girl had whacked him, and I'd love to see that happen.'

'I won't be telling anyone in a hurry, mate,' Jamie shrugged. 'There is no way I'm having that smelly bastard on top of me again. Let him tell his stories we know what really happened, and that's all that matters.'

She got to her feet and said her goodbyes. The spliff had given her the calm she needed to face Michael and luckily it was only him at home sat in front of the TV, channel hopping. She took her jacket off and threw it over the chair before sitting down next to him.

'Hey, Mikey, what you watching?' The silence seemed forever. 'We need to talk about stuff, mate, we can't leave it like this.'

Before she could explain, he threw the remote control at the TV and it landed in pieces. Jamie tried to sound convincing, but Michael wasn't taking anything in.

'Mikey, it's all over, they won't bother you again. Ricky told them I was with him.'

Michael scoffed sarcastically at Jamie's comment and almost spat his words in her face.

'If you think people are going to fall for that bullshit, you must be the stupidest dyke on the planet.'

'Look, mate, I'm sorry that you got a beating because of me, I feel terrible and if it's any consolation, I had a beating myself yesterday and if it weren't for Ricky, I'd probably be in the hospital now, or worse so I know what you're going through.'

Michael wasn't going to let her off lightly he was too wired for apologies.

'Well, that's your own fault, how could you have been so stupid to let Martin see you! My life is shit, Sis, and I have enough to put up with without half the fucking neighbourhood chasing me around and calling me a queer.' He rose to his feet and towered over Jamie. 'You've really fucked up this time, and if Dad finds out about this, he'll probably kick you out. That's if he doesn't kill you first.'

He was right, and she knew it.

'I'm sorry—this had nothing to do with you. I don't know why they had to pick on you, anyway.'

He kicked the door in anger, then bounded back towards her.

'They've been after me for ages, you silly twat, they just wanted a valid reason to do it. Why do you think they have such a problem with queers? 'She shrugged her shoulders and Mikey explained. 'It's because Kevin Thompson can't handle the fact that he's a poof.'

'What! —you're joking how do you know all this?'

'It's not a fucking joke Jamie, he's a poof. Don't ask me how I know—I just do, and he will stop at nothing to hide the fact.'

Jamie turned off the TV and closed the door. She kept one eye on Michael and the other on the front window. She didn't want her parents walking in on them talking.

'You must have got this wrong Mikey, they would have raped me last night if Ricky hadn't stopped them.'

'Sis, you have to believe me, he likes to play the straight man in front of his brother—Jesus, I can't believe I'm telling you all this.'

'That's bullshit! You must have the wrong boy, why would he tell you he's gay? He's a fucking psycho.'

Michael stood up and paced the floor. He was shaking with anger at Jamie's disbelief of him; his face red with a temper.

'For the last time, he's gay. I know and do you know how I know—because I fucked him.'

Jamie was gobsmacked. This was so unexpected. She hadn't a clue about Michael. She had been so wrapped up in her own sexuality she had never noticed that her little brother was going through the same turmoil.

'You can close your mouth, Jamie. It can't have been that much of a shock, surely.'

He sat back down, relieved that he had finally told someone. 'Now, do you believe me about Kevin?' Jamie nodded her head. 'He was taunting me around school for months calling me a mummy's boy and then I caught him looking at me in the shower after football. Later that day, he cornered me and made me give him a blow job behind the garages. I didn't mind, it stopped him bullying me. So, whenever he wants a bit of cock, he comes to find me.'

'Mikey—I had no idea, honest bro.'

'Why should you? I was doing a pretty good job of hiding it until you got caught with your hands in some girls' pants. You've got to be more careful sis if Dad finds out we're both dead.'

Jamie didn't know whether to be happy about the news or cry. She was so worried that her brother wouldn't accept her as a lesbian, she hadn't entertained the fact that the problem had been about her getting caught. At least she didn't have to worry about Michael telling her parents about what had happened, so that was one fear she could safely put to bed. She thanked Michael for his honesty, apologised yet again for her carelessness, and left Michael trying to fix the remote control.

Chapter 9

Jamie arrived earlier than expected and Abi showed her in through the kitchen. Hundreds of tiny teapots lined the Welsh Dresser shelves, just waiting for Jamie to knock them off with her rucksack. She waded through as carefully as she could in a sheer panic of what treasures may lay ahead.

She felt a little awkward with it being just the two of them as she didn't know Abi that well. She wasn't that confident with small talk either, so she was a little taken aback when the girl had questions.

'So how long have you known that you like girls? Or is this just a Heather thing?'

Although shocked, she was also a little impressed that she could be so upfront and finished taking the cans of Special out of her rucksack. Ricky had sold them to her earlier in the evening along with some dope, just enough to get her through the weekend.

'I suppose I've always known that I was different but didn't know why it's not that I don't like boys—I just don't like them—like that.'

'Heather likes you a lot. She told me what happened the other night. I couldn't believe it, she said that making love with Dexter had never made her feel like that, she said that with you she just lost all control.'

The words making love with Dexter hit Jamie like a slap in the face. Heather had told her they had never slept together. It wouldn't have made any difference to her if they had done, so there was no need for her to lie about it. This irritated Jamie. She hated being lied to more than anything. She was nobody's mug, and as the frustration grew, she contemplated leaving.

'Is that a can of lager I see poking out of your bag chick?' Abi had clocked it and Jamie felt a bit embarrassed by its presence.

'Yeah—sorry mate, I should have asked you first if it was OK to bring some.'

Abi pulled the can the rest of the way out and cracked it open. 'It's always OK to bring some babe. You just have to make sure you know how to share.'

As she tugged the rest of the cans out of her rucksack, the block of dope fell out onto the floor. They both bent down to pick it up, but Abi got there first. She twisted it around in her fingers.

'Is this what I think it is?'

'Yeah shit—sorry again, I should never have brought it to your house,' she got up to leave 'I'll just go I'm not being fair on you.'

'Don't be daft, Heather and I used to smoke it all the time when I was with Izzy.'

Izzy was Abi's ex-boyfriend he was a lot older than her and a bit of a weirdo. She rolled the dope around in her hands, then tossed it back at Jamie.

'So maybe we could share some later—yeah?'

'Yeah—maybe.'

Jamie was a bit shocked that Heather had ever taken drugs she thought that she was too squeaky clean for all that. There seemed to be a lot she didn't know, and this was unnerving her.

'So, Abi, you and Heather have been friends a long time, did she ever mention that she liked girls?'

'Not really—but she dragged me to your house one time, and I didn't quite understand why. She told me you had a book she wanted to borrow, but when we got to your street, she changed her mind. How lame was that? Maybe if she had plucked up the courage to knock on your door, you guys would have got together a lot sooner. It is hard for her with Dex and her parents, they control her life. She'll never be able to finish with him. They wouldn't allow it. Sad really, but at least she has you to take her mind off things.'

Jamie didn't like the idea of him still hanging around and was wondering if the story that Heather had told her about her wanting them to finish was entirely true.

The phone rang, and Abi went inside to answer it. Jamie could hear Abi's raised voice but couldn't quite work out what she was saying. Two minutes later she came back into the room.

'Bad news, I'm afraid. That was Heather's dad on the phone. Her pig of a boyfriend has told him what happened at school, and that you and she were getting over-friendly. She's denied it, but her dad preferred to believe Dexter as usual. She's grounded and been told never to speak to the likes of you again.' Abi paused to let Jamie take it all in. 'Her mam and dad are religious freaks, and that sort of thing won't be tolerated in their family—his words babe, not mine. He wanted to know if I knew anything about you? But I told him that Dex was lying and that Heather only knew you from school. Sorry babes you two are not getting much of a break at all are you?'

She could feel the rage inviting her face to redden. 'What the fuck does that spoilt little brat know about anything? He's probably had his mummy and daddy wiping his arse for him all of his life. He knows nothing about the real world—And who does Mr fucking Gardner think he is judging me before he's even met me!'

Abi rubbed her hand up and down Jamie's arm 'Don't take it to heart, they are all the same these religious freaks telling you that you'll burn in hell for wearing your skirt too high and makeup is the devil's work. It's pathetic. It's just another threat to keep us all in line.'

Jamie shook her head in disbelief. 'That boy is such an arsehole, though. We saw him this morning before school and how I never pulled his fucking underpants over his head, I don't know. He's a total loser. What does she see in him?' Jamie reached over and grabbed her coat. 'I'd better pack my things up and leave you in peace, all this shit must be doing your head in.'

Jamie repacked her rucksack and pulled it on her back.

'Don't go yet—stay for a while and chill. You promised me half of that stuff, remember? It will all blow over by tomorrow, and she'll be back with Dexter, making her parents happy and seeing you when she can.'

Jamie didn't want to be someone's dirty little secret, but she knew what Abi meant. She dropped her bag back to the floor and got out her tobacco tin. After carefully rolling up a spliff, she went outside to the back garden to smoke it. She nodded back at Abi to join her.

'Crack open another couple of cans for us to go with this and you're on.'

Abi brought out the beer and sat on the wall. They passed the spliff back and forth to each other. Each of them holding the draw for as long as they could till the burn in the back of their throats took hold. The effect was almost instantaneous, and the two girls were loosening up.

'So, what's happening in Abi's life then, is Izzy still on the scene?'

'Nah, babe, that finished a long time ago. I'm happy on my own I don't need all that drama with the exams coming up. There's no way I'm gonna spend another year in that dump of a school. As soon as I get my qualifications, I'm off. Aren't you worried about what will happen to us when we leave school?'

Jamie looked at the floor. She had hated school since the second year.

Mrs Rogers the English teacher had embarrassed her in front of the class about her uniform being untidy. She had tried her best to look after herself and keep clean. But there's not a lot you can do if you have holes in your shoes and your uniform is two sizes too small, she thought.

'I'm hardly ever there, so it's not gonna make much of a difference to me, and I can't see any of the teachers letting me take my exams as most of them don't even know my name.'

Abi downed the last of her can and took another drag on the spliff.

'Miss Halliwell knows your name,' she giggled 'I've seen the way you stare at her in class. Oh Yes, Miss Halliwell—anything I can do for you, Miss Halliwell? —can I shag the pants off you, Miss Halliwell?' She sniggered. 'She's a bit old for you, isn't she?'

'Shut the fuck up. Weirdo Lover.' She gave Abi a gentle slap across the back of her head. 'What would you know? She's as sexy as fuck—and she's only in her twenty's, that's not old.' After taking the spliff back, she inhaled the last drag and stubbed it out on the floor.

'You'd better chuck that over the wall before you come back in here. If my Gran finds it, she'll have a heart attack on the spot.'

Jamie did as she requested, and both girls went back inside the house.

They downed the rest of the cans during the evening, and everything seemed funny to them now. Even the boring TV advertisements had them rolling around in hysteria. But Jamie was still feeling confused.

'Abi—can I ask you something about Heather?'

'Yeah, sure babe, what do you want to know?'

'Well, if she's sleeping with Dex, and she's never gonna leave him. Then what the fuck is she doing with me?'

Abi put a caring arm around her new friend. 'Who knows? It's obvious that she fancies the pants off you, and if I were into girls, you would definitely be my first choice. Maybe you should just enjoy it while it lasts.'

Abi's arm stayed locked around Jamie's shoulder as they continued drinking and laughing at the TV. As she leaned forward to pick up her can, Abi's hand slid down her back to the top of her jeans. The two girls were getting easy with each other and as Jamie leaned back to her sitting position Abi seized the moment and kissed Jamie. She responded for a few seconds, then to Abi's disappointment, Jamie pulled away.

'Hey Abs, it's not that I don't like you—I really do—It's just Heather y'know.'

Abi felt really embarrassed by her actions but knew that she didn't regret it. Although she and Heather were best friends, she felt an urge far greater than friendship breaking through the barrier. The mixture of drugs and alcohol was taking over and the ability to control her wanting was hard to keep at bay.

'I'm sorry babe, I shouldn't have—you're right.'

She looked into Abi's eyes and saw a hunger that was very much like her own. With the thought of Heather lying to her about Dexter overtaking her rational thinking, she let go of her inhibitions and encouraged Abi's intentions.

They both had had way too much to drink and felt stoned as hell. Abi got up and dragged Jamie by the hand to lead her upstairs. Their bodies pressed tightly together as they tried to walk and kiss at the same time. Stopping at the bottom and looking hungrily into each other's eyes, they knew that as soon as they started there was no going back. This wasn't a love thing, this was a pure lust for both of them. Just a means to satisfy an end.

Whilst trying to make their way up the stairs to the bedroom, Jamie stopped. Her patience was wearing thin. She ripped off Abi's skirt and began kissing the inside of her thighs, slowly at first, then biting her way to the top of her legs. Abi grabbed Jamie's hair so tightly that she let out a loud groan of excitement and pain. Abi lifted her legs to hook Jamie's neck, and as she tried to resist her, she grabbed at the stair carpet with both hands.

She manoeuvred Abi the rest of the way to the bedroom and placed her onto the bed. She kissed her
deeply, but as Abi undid Jamie's shirt she gasped as
she noticed the imprint from the studded belt that had
remained on her pure white skin. Jamie had forgotten
about her brand mark in all the passion and quickly but-
toned up her shirt.

'I'm sorry—I can't do this.' She took Abi by surprise,
'we shouldn't have...'

Jamie felt a sudden pang of guilt as she remembered
what she had gone through to get this far. She quickly
tidied herself up and ran down the stairs before Abi had
a chance to comment about her injuries.

She hurried into the room to get her boots and jacket.
She thought of how different it would have turned out
if Heather had turned up. As she opened the front door,
she heard Abi's call. With guilt about leaving on her
mind, she turned to see Abi standing at the top of the
stairs, wrapped in just a bedsheet.

'Jamie, stop, it's really late—you don't have to leave.
I won't tell anyone about this—it never happened, OK.
Just come back and calm down.'

Jamie paused for a second without turning around,
then shut the door as Abi continued.

'Just give me five minutes to take a shower and I'll be
down, just don't go anywhere OK.'

Jamie went back into the living room and waited. She
still had the taste of Abi on her lips and felt bad about

storming off, but no matter how she tried, Heather was still the face she saw when she closed her eyes.

After a short while, a fully dressed Abi returned to the room and Jamie felt reluctant to look at her.

'Listen, babe, to be honest, I was feeling a little guilty myself—and this was all my fault, I led you on. I haven't been with anyone since Izzy, and I don't know what came over me. It was a heat of the moment thing—and as I said, no one has to know. We can blame the spliff, and just keep it between us...'

'I really do like you Abi, you're gorgeous and I shouldn't have taken advantage of your friendship but...'

'Did you hear me complaining? —um no. So, stop beating yourself up about it. I'll get you a blanket and you can sleep down here if you like. Maybe we'll talk about it tomorrow, or maybe we won't—whatever you feel like doing is fine by me. Now get some sleep.'

* * *

The postman came early, and his delivery woke Jamie with a startle. Not that she had gotten much sleep the night before. She had the hangover from hell and so many regrets about what had happened between her and Abi that she knew she'd have a problem facing either of the girls again. She grabbed her things together and left before Abi got up.

The fresh morning air hit her as she started her journey home, and she was thinking of a way to get to see Heather and face her straight on. She knew that Abi wouldn't mention what had happened between them, so with a bit of luck, she might just get away with it. The fact that she had a few questions about Dexter that she would like answering didn't excuse her behaviour with Abi and she knew it. She took a walk past Heather's house discreetly to see if she could catch a glimpse, but the place seemed empty, so she just carried on home.

As she walked onto the street, she noticed two police cars parked outside Ricky's house. She wasn't surprised, as she knew that one of Ricky's older brothers had been seen plain as day on a security camera earlier in the week. He had been stealing bricks from the building site behind the bowling alley to sell on to a cowboy builder. She giggled to herself, thinking of the excuses that were going to be given to the police from the Webster's. They were so good at making up elaborate fairy stories to cover each other's actions that they were almost believable.

As Jamie entered her house, she saw her dad sitting at the kitchen table reading his paper, so she closed the door softly and began to climb the stairs.

'Get back down here, young lady—I want a word with you. Where do you think you've been all bloody night? Well?'

Jamie shrugged her shoulders in her usual way.

'I've had some posh geezer round yer' saying that you've been harassing his daughter, is it true?'

Jamie's heart started pounding in fear. She wanted to run, but she knew that would make her look guilty, so she took a deep breath and turned on the stairs.

'What! I haven't got a clue what you're talking about.'

'Don't give me that look Jamie girl, I always know when you're lying. So where have you been all night? You might as well tell me cos you know I'll find out.'

She could feel her mouth drying up and bit her lip. 'I've been with Ricky—we were playing on his Nintendo and we fell asleep.'

Jamie had to think on her feet and hoped he would believe her. She knew with the police cars outside he wouldn't check, but that didn't stop him getting angry and giving her a quick slap across the back of her head.

'I told you not to hang around with that boy, he and his father are both useless wasters. The whole family are a bunch of scrounging Irish Gypsies—stay away from them, do you hear?' He moved in closer, inches away from her face. 'So, about this girl, what have you been up to?'

She wiped her father's spit off her face with her sleeve, 'Nothing Dad, honest I don't know what you're talking about.'

He gave her another slap, this time so hard that she landed on the kitchen chair. He pulled the chair towards him and pointed in her face.

'Don't fucking lie to me girl, you're just like your mother always trying to wind me up. It makes me so fucking angry! Now I'm fed up of repeating myself.' He paced around the kitchen for a while then pointed back in her face. 'Her old man said that you had been trying to force yourself on her like a dirty fucking lezza. So, help me god there will be nothing like that in this fucking house. Do you understand?'

Jamie rubbed the back of her aching head, but still denied it. She ducked his final blow and bolted through the back door, stumbling as she ran. She glanced back to see if her dad was following, there was no sign of him for now, but she knew it wouldn't be long. She looked over at the Websters house. The police cars were still outside so no point running over to Ricky. She decided the safest thing to do would be to go back to Abi's and hide out there for a while until he'd calmed down or passed out from drinking. At least there she could hatch some sort of plan to get out of the situation she had regrettably put herself in. If not, she would have to get as far away from her own father as possible.

When she arrived at Abi's house, it shocked her to see who answered the door.

'Heather, I thought they had grounded you. Christ, your father is not in there, is he?' she poked her head through to look.

'No, but he will be in an hour or so. He's only let me out to help Abi with the garden.'

Her father had quizzed her all night trying to get to the truth about Jamie, and she was only allowed to Abi's house to fulfil a promise. The girls had promised to tidy the garden while the old lady was away for the weekend, and her dad had driven her there to do just that. She was to call him as soon as they had finished, and he would pick her up.

Heather led the way straight passed Abi. As she disappeared into the room, Jamie took the opportunity to whisper to her partner in crime.

'Abi is it OK if I have a quiet word with Heather, I know it's awkward but...'

'Sh, I told you no one has to know about us, go and sort it out with your girlfriend babe.'

As Jamie entered the room, Heather flung her arms around her, hugging her tightly while apologising for her father's behaviour.

'I tried to tell him, but he wouldn't listen, I'm so sorry that he went to your house.'

Jamie pushed Heather away to an arm's length. 'He doesn't realise what he's started. My father is nothing like yours he doesn't take kindly to visitors, especially ones with news about his family. I'm surprised your dad didn't get a mouthful or more really Heather.'

'He did say that your dad looked like he was about to explode.'

Jamie shook her head from side to side. 'He did explode, and he would kill me literally. You don't know what he's like, this is all fucked up now—again!'

Jamie turned her back on Heather. She couldn't look into her dishonest eyes.

'Why did you lie to me Heather, about sleeping with Dexter? It would have made no difference to me, everyone is sleeping with their boyfriends at our age, you really didn't have to keep it from me.'

'Dexter tells everyone that we are sleeping together Jamie, he doesn't want his friends to label him a virgin. I haven't lied to you, I swear, you are the only one I have ever got that close to.'

'This has nothing to do with Dexter, Heather, I know you've been lying to me, I can't explain why but I know.'

Abi had been listening outside the door and couldn't let Jamie feel like she had to cover up for her. So, she came in to explain.

'Heather, it was me that told her, sorry babe, I didn't know it was a secret and it just came out as we were talking. I would never have betrayed your confidence like that, we have been friends for too long, please forgive me.'

Abi had wanted forgiveness from her best friend for what had happened last night as well, but vowed she would never find out about it from her. It would only make things worse if Heather knew about their intoxicated liaison, she thought. So, it would be best all-round if they just forget that it had ever happened.

Heather felt awkward and wished the ground would swallow her up. She looked at the two girls stood in front of her and couldn't hide her embarrassment.

'Sit down both, I have a bit of a confession to make. I'm sorry Abi, I have lied, but not to Jamie, to you.' The confusion on their faces was apparent.

'A few months ago, we were having a sleepover at Shelly's house. Do you remember?'

'Yes, but—I don't understand.'

'Well, that night we were all confiding in each other about how we felt the first time we made love. You and Shelly are far more experienced than me, and I felt like a fool as—I hadn't ever slept with anyone. I'm sorry Abi it was a stupid thing to lie about and I've never lied to you before, but I just felt so out of place.'

Abi hugged her best friend and as she did, she looked over to Jamie ashamedly.

'Don't worry, Heather, we've all added a little more spice to our lives to take them up a level—even me. I've definitely done things that I shouldn't have, it's just sometimes your feelings run away with you, and there's not a lot you can do to stop it. I'll leave you and Jamie alone for a while to talk things through. I'll be upstairs if you need me.'

Heather's confession had filled Jamie with regret. If she hadn't had felt so betrayed by Heather, she would have probably left last night to look for her. Instead, she was jumping all over her best friend, and doubting Heather's every word.

Jamie held her girl close as she breathed in and out deeply. She trusted Abi when she said that she would never tell, but the guilt inside her would never go away.

Learning to live with it was her only option. She hated secrets but couldn't see any other way out.

'I'm sorry for ever doubting you, Heather. I should have known that you wouldn't be the type to lie. My life is so crazy, and I have a lot of things to deal with at home, things you would never believe. I'm not really that good at trusting people either. When something good happens in my life there is always a consequence to pay.'

'Do you think it's worth me talking to your dad about all this?' Heather said calmly. 'I could explain that my father had heard it wrong and falsely accused you.'

That was the last thing she needed if Heather met Jamie Senior that would put an end to their relationship. He would probably be his usual bullying self and verbally attack her for wasting his time. Or take a trip out on the warpath looking for Heather's father to teach him a lesson for slagging off his daughter, she thought. Even though he was a terrible father, if an outsider tried to reprimand his kids, he would always come to their defence. This time, though, her father had suspicions that were founded. He had thought all his life that Jamie wasn't quite the pretty little girl she was meant to be, and she knew it. They would need a more calculated approach if she were going to save her skin this time, she thought.

'What we need is for Dexter to say he was lying, the only thing is, how are we gonna get him to do it?' The cogs in Jamie's brain started turning. 'We could always threaten him with someone or blackmail him even.'

Heather had an idea. 'Dexter has a little secret of his own that he wouldn't want his mates finding out about.'

'Well, don't keep us in suspense, what's the plan?' Jamie said impatiently.

'Well, it's obvious really, he's told everyone that we've slept together, so I'll tell him that if he doesn't put things right, I'll tell his mates he's a virgin, that would kill him, he'd be a laughingstock, he couldn't cope with that following him around.'

Jamie raised an eyebrow. 'It's got to be worth a try.'

'Brilliant, I'll give him a ring now and see how he feels about being pushed into a corner.'

Heather shouted upstairs to Abi 'Can I use your phone? We have a plan.'

Abi turned the TV off upstairs and came down to meet them both. 'Yeah, babe, go ahead, you know where it is.'

As Heather left the room, Jamie took an uneasy look towards Abi.

'Is it OK if I go out the back for a smoke?'

'Yeah—hang on, I'll follow you out.'

The two girls felt embarrassed to be in each other's company, especially sober.

'How long has Heather been here?'

'Not long—she doesn't know that you stayed here last night she thinks that you left straight after the phone call, I thought it best not to say.'

'Thanks, you're right it would have led to a few complicated questions, and I've enough shit to deal with at the moment. I'm really sorry for reacting the way I did yesterday, I shouldn't have freaked out like that.'

'Don't worry about it babe, it's all forgotten,' Abi tried to explain herself without sounding harsh. 'I don't mean forgotten as in—I want to forget it—as in I didn't enjoy it. I really did.'

'Enjoy what?' Heather ambled through the door and sat on the wall next to Jamie.

'It doesn't matter—did you get through to the little scrote? Is he gonna sort things out with your dad?'

'Well, after he called me all the names under the sun, threatened to take back all the CD's he has ever bought me and insisted that I must be mad to be friends with someone like you—he agreed. He said he would only do it if I go with him later tonight to the bowling alley.'

'But you can't you're grounded.'

'That's what I said, but he said if I ask my dad to drop us both off he would explain to him beforehand. He's going to say that he misread the signs and, in a bid, to protect my reputation, he jumped to a conclusion too quickly.'

Jamie jumped off the wall and stood in front of Heather. 'Hang on a minute, why does he want you to go to the bowling alley, he's not expecting to take you out on a date after what he has done, surely?'

'He said that his mates are going to be there tonight, and he wants to finish with me in front of them, so he doesn't look like an idiot in school when people find out about our friendship.'

'That's ridiculous, he's paranoid—I'm coming with you...'

'No, he said that if he sees you there, he will tell my dad that I pleaded with him to lie about the truth. I have to go alone it's the only way out of all this.'

Heather held Jamie's hand. 'Don't worry, I'll be OK I've spent many a boring night at that bowling alley with Dexter another one won't kill me.'

Jamie pulled her girl close and stroked her face gently, 'OK but be careful you know what his mouth is like, he wants people to think that he's the big I am, not the tiny little nothing that everybody knows he is.'

'Jamie this will work out, I promise, then when it's over we can concentrate on us, and that's all I want to think about right now, apart from this garden. If my dad comes around checking and it's not done, I'll be in a whole heap of trouble and I need to stay on his good side until tonight.'

'Well, I'd better make myself scarce if I'm going to be around after the bowling tonight. As long as I can keep out of my dad's way, I should survive.'

Chapter 10

On the way to the bowling alley, Heather kept her gaze firmly out of the car window. Thinking back on how Dexter had explained to her dad that it was all one big misunderstanding made her stomach sour. His whiny voice full of lies made her regret all the times she had had to put up with him for the sake of her family. All those times that she had spent wishing she was somewhere else. She couldn't believe that even after all the upset he caused yesterday, her dad was still treating him as the blue-eyed boy and that Heather was allowed on a date with him.

Jamie had kept her distance, just as she had promised, but wasn't far away. Ricky had to go to the building site behind the bowling alley in a search to find his brother's drugs, so she tagged along to lend a watchful eye. When the police caught his brother stealing from there, he threw the stash in wild panic and hadn't yet had the chance to retrieve them. So, she offered to help with the search.

'Maybe the builders have already found them, Rick?'

'Well, judging by the state of that brickwork over there Jay, you may be right girl.'

Jamie laughed for the first time in ages, Ricky may have been a bad boy, but he always had a wicked sense of humour. She had told him earlier about Dexter stirring things with her father. He hated snobby little runts like him, so had hatched a plan of his own. He didn't give Jamie all the details, just told her he'd planned a little surprise for the squealer, so she knew that she'd get revenge on him one way or another.

They started moving around the rubble, taking care to avoid the security cameras.

'Lift that tarpaulin back Jay and see if it's fallen through the planks, your hands are smaller than mine, you might be able to reach it.'

As she pulled back the sheet, a rat ran out from under it towards Ricky and he let out a high-pitched scream.

'Aargh—what the fuck was that?' he jumped on to the wall behind him in a blind panic.'

Jamie couldn't control herself and fell about laughing. 'You wimp Ricky Webster, it was only a baby.'

'You won't be saying that when he's scratching you with his little baby claws and sinking his little baby teeth into the side of your leg, that's for sure, fuck it! —fuck it!—I hate them, scary little bastards, I don't want to play anymore.'

As usual for a Saturday, the bowling alley was packed with the kids from school. Dexter had already booked ahead to make sure he had the lane with the best view of the balcony where he knew his friends would be standing. As he walked towards them, he quickly went over his demands with Heather.

'Right—we pretend to argue, I'll shout out I'm finishing with you and you storm off really upset—got it?'

'Dex there's no need for all of this why do you always care what people think of you? Can't we just split up like everyone else? All this need to make a big scene it's crazy.'

'We can always forget it, Heather and I'll pay another visit to your parent's house. I'm sure your little girlfriend would get on well with your dad and his church activities. How would you like that?'

Heather gave Dexter a scornful look.

'Well, just shut it then Heather, we had a deal. This is all your fault, remember.'

Heather looked around, happy that she couldn't see Jamie watching how this prick was treating her. This was all for them to have a chance of a relationship, and she had to keep that thought firmly in mind. As Dexter pushed past her to grab the best bowling ball, she felt like hitting him on the head with hers but began the game instead. Regardless of the need to win, she rolled her ball down the lane, aiming it for the side gully.

'For Christ's sake, Heather, can't you do anything right?' Dexter shouted as he pushed Heather out of the way to take his turn. 'I'm fed up with you always showing me up in public.'

He took a glance over to his friends standing on the balcony, to make sure they were watching and more importantly listening. He only had one chance at this, so he wanted to make sure it was a good one raising his voice to get the attention he needed.

'I know you've begged me a million times to stay with you, but I don't think it's working out anymore I think we should finish it now. I'm just not interested in you anymore—you disgust me.'

He bent down to pick up his bowling ball and was glad that he had got his statement heard by everyone that he thought mattered. Most of his friends were as pretentious as him, and a couple even smirked when they heard Dexter's words. As he straightened himself back up and held his ball out in front of him, he could feel someone standing close behind him, so close that he could feel their breath on the back of his neck. He didn't want to turn around, and as the voice from behind him boomed in his ear he jumped shockingly not knowing what to expect.

'Well, that's not a very nice way to talk to a lady now is it Dexter old boy. Forgive him Miss Gardner what he meant to say is he's not interested in you anymore because he's a bum boy ain't you Dexter?'

He turned around to see the Thompson brother's standing either side of him.

'We know all about you mate from Ricky Webster he said that they saw you giving head to a sixth-form boy in the locker room.'

'What! That's ridiculous Ricky who?'

'You know who we're talking about, mate, so don't try to get out of it.'

Dexter took another look over at his friends. They had all turned their backs away from the alley, pretending to engage in idle conversation. When the Thompson boys were around, it was always best not to get involved and everyone knew that.

Dexter tried once more to get the attention of his friends on the balcony by shouting over to them.

'Guys—guys I'm as straight as you are,' he couldn't believe that they had abandoned them. He then turned and pleaded with Heather, 'tell them that you're my girl-friend, go on, tell them.'

Heather knew only too well what the Thompson boys were capable of, she had seen it for herself first-hand with Michael. She hated Dexter for what he said about her, but still didn't want to see him being beaten to a pulp by these thugs. As she went to open her mouth to defend him, Wayne Thompson put his arm around her shoulder and pulled her close to him.

'She's not your girlfriend mate, we just heard you fin-ish with her. She's a pretty girl Dexter what's the mat-ter with you? No decent straight man would chuck her back on the shelf so there must be something wrong with you.'

'Heather, tell these losers that we've been together for years, there's no way I'm gay.'

He looked over again for the support of his so-called friends.

'Lads we've been chums since primary school, please, tell them I'm not gay.'

None of them dared to look over. It seemed that this mummy's boy wasn't worth the hassle to anyone.

When Dexter realised he had no backup, he feared for the consequences. He took small steps backwards, then threw his bowling ball at the brothers. He had a queue of kids in front of him, all waiting for their shoe collection, but he pushed himself through by jumping over them. The ones on the floor that were randomly putting their shoes on moaned as he stepped all over them, crushing tiny little toes in haste. The parents of the smaller ones shouted abuse at him as he rushed on by. This helped the brothers in their pursuit.

He ran through the complex frantically looking left to right for a quick escape, but it was too busy, so he tried his luck through the fast-food hall. As there was only one entrance, he jumped over a booth and locked himself in the girl's toilets.

The Thompson boys weren't far behind him, they were dragging Heather along too. A security guard was talking to a girl at the entrance of the girl's toilets and as the boy's looked around to catch sight of Dexter, they overheard the girl explaining that some boy had just pushed his way through the queue and locked himself in the stall, as the other toilets in there were out of order the queue of teenage girls were shouting and screaming at him to get out. Wayne Thompson smiled as he saw the security guard doing the job of getting Dexter out of the toilets for him amongst a gaggle of angry teenage girls.

Dexter was forcefully escorted off the premises by two large security guards and the brothers waited until they were firmly out of the way before going back inside to start the chase again. They dropped Heather as the extra baggage was making too much noise and was attracting too much attention.

By ducking in between and crawling under cars, Dexter had disappeared out of sight. They asked the restless crowd outside if anyone had seen him and luckily; someone had spotted him climbing over the fence and running towards the building site. Jamie and Ricky had also seen Dexter. They were sitting up on the scaffolding at the far end of the site with a couple of cans for company. They watched him hastily scramble his way over the rubble with the Thompson boys closing in on him.

'See, I told you I'd sort it.'

Ricky was pleased with himself now and was enjoying the game of cat and mouse that was happening in front of him.

'Fuck, where's Heather? This is dodgy Rick, she was supposed to be with him tonight to sort things out.'

'Well, she's not with him now, so don't worry—just enjoy the show.'

Jamie saw movement out of the corner of her eye and leaned over to get a better look at the rear entrance gate. It was Heather. She had made her way around the outside of the fence. Jamie scrambled to her feet to get to her before anyone else. She climbed down the scaffolding and crept her way towards her.

'What are you doing here?' Heather shouted towards Jamie, but luckily the boys were still too far away to hear her.

'Sh, get your arse over here before we're next on the fucking list.'

Jamie helped Heather climb the scaffolding and stayed in the shadows, out of sight. She had to put her hand over Heather's mouth to keep her quiet as the screams from Dexter echoed throughout the building site. The Thompson brothers had really laid into him. This was too frightening to watch, even for Ricky. The boys had left him naked, wet and face down in the sand with cuts and bruises all over him. Jamie could see a twinge of guilt in Ricky's eyes as he climbed down the scaffolding, but she knew he would never admit it.

'He got what he deserved, Jay. Your father would have given you much the same if he'd had carried on with his big mouth and you know it.'

Heather looked over to Jamie, her face wet with tears.

'What does he mean, Jamie? Your father wouldn't do something like that to you, would he?'

Ricky raised his eyebrows and confirmed his statement.

'You haven't met Jamie's mother yet, have you? Maybe you should ask her that question.'

As Ricky manoeuvred himself on to the lower level, he lost his footing and fell onto the deck below.

'Rick, are you OK mate?' Jamie leaned over the side to see if he was alright.

'Yeah, I'm OK Jay I just landed on my arse that's all.'

As he pulled himself up, he saw a blue carrier bag hanging off the outer scaffolding pole.

'Yey, Jamie, I've found the stash whoop whoop.'

He edged his way forward to reach for the bag, but as he grabbed it, the plank underneath him gave way. He tried to grab for the pole as he went down but couldn't reach it. The builders had dug a trench and had filled it with rubble ready for a cement drop. Ricky hit his head on the side of the digger before falling headfirst into the hole. Blood flowed out of Ricky's lifeless body as it lay twisted at the bottom of the pile. The blue carrier bag that had taken his young life still clutched in his hand.

* * *

The day of the funeral ironically coincided with the arrest of the Thompson brothers. After a brief stay in the hospital, Dexter had regained consciousness and told the police everything. Jamie and Heather had kept quiet about the whole ordeal as when they left the building site to get help for Ricky, a police car passed them at the entrance and headed straight for the site. They hoped that they would find Ricky's body and see that it was an accident, that way they wouldn't have to explain to their parents what had happened.

One of Dexter's friends must have had a pang of guilt at the time and informed the police about the Thompson brothers. They were told that they were last seen heading towards the building site and that Dexter's life would probably be in danger if they didn't hurry.

They found Ricky's body shortly after, and because he had a lot of drugs and alcohol in his system, this led them to believe that it was death by misadventure, so there was no need for any further enquiry into how he died.

Jamie stood in her front room looking out of the window over at the Webster's house. She still couldn't believe that her one loyal friend in all the world had gone. As the funeral cars arrived, she remembered how the two of them had said that they would get off the estate when she turned sixteen and set up a place together in the city. Ricky had always wanted to open a second-hand record stall in the market, he collected old records and CDs of just about anything. He had extended his record collection by luck at the end of last year.

It was the night before Christmas Eve, and Jamie and Ricky had been trying to break into garages for aerosols and glue to get a buzz off. They had broken an old lock off one with a crowbar. Inside, they found boxes of old singles stashed among crates of alcohol. The boxes had the words 'Pub Juke Box' written on them, and the collection was right up to date with the chart stuff. Knowing it would take ages to carry away on foot, they roped Ricky's dad into helping them steal it with his van. Ricky's dad knew where it had come from originally, as he knew of a club in town that had recently suffered a hit. He thought that whoever did it had made a stupid mistake hiding it in a garage on an estate. It still made Jamie smile to think what the thieves' faces must have looked like when they opened the garage, and the stuff was gone. They couldn't exactly report it to the police, so nobody found out, and they were in the clear. They had spent an entire three months intoxicated with the stuff. Ricky would throw down bottles of cider out of his bedroom window for her any time that she asked, and he had the record collection he had always wanted.

'Are you ready to go, Sis?'

Michael stood behind her in his smart black suit.

'It's just that the cars will leave soon, and we should get over there.'

Jamie hadn't cried right until that moment, and as the tears poured down her face, her brother put his arm around her as they made their way through the front door.

The next few hours seemed a blur. Heather had been expected to turn up for the funeral, but for some reason or another, she had thought better of it. Jamie hadn't seen her much since that night and thought that the drama of it all had scared her away. But the truth of the matter would have been harder to handle as Heather had found out about Jamie and Abi's little encounter.

The day after the accident, Heather confided in Abi about their presence at the building site and repeated what Ricky had told her about Jamie's dad hitting her mother. The girls were getting concerned for Jamie's safety and Abi commented without thinking about the scar that Jamie had across her chest and wondered whether her father was to blame for it being there. Heather had never seen the scar and wanted to know the truth about how *she* had seen it, so cornered Abi into confessing. But no matter how hard Abi pleaded with Heather to make her understand that it was all a big mistake, Heather couldn't forgive them. She had decided not to confront Jamie about it out of respect for the mourning of Ricky, instead; she would stay away and forget that there ever was a Jamie Taylor.

Ricky's father had found his salvation at the bottom of a bottle. He didn't want his emotions to be shown as a sign of weakness and kept his grief to himself as much as he could. This was the opposite of Ricky's mother. She was busying herself around asking people if they wanted more food at least twice in the same minute. The pills she had taken were enough to knock out a gorilla and yet she still walked the floor with her trays of food, wide-eyed and in a trance. She called her other sons by

Ricky's name each time one of them spoke to her and didn't have the strength to correct herself. It would be a long time before the Webster household would return to being the crazy place of noise and laughter that it once was.

'I think we should leave now Sis, you look shattered and Dad said that he wanted us home as soon as it finished, you know what he's like about us being here in the first place.'

'Bollocks to him, Michael. You can go if you want to but I'm staying here I'm fed up with his fucking rules. He's probably pissed and out cold on the floor by now, anyway.'

Jamie cracked open another can and went into the kitchen to talk to Ricky's dad.

As she sat down next to him, she could see how the lack of sleep had affected the poor man; eyes red with harboured tears hung heavy over the black bags that etched his face. He looked up at her and half-smiled.

'How's your mam, Jamie? Has that eejit of a father of yours stopped using her as a sparring partner yet?' He took a large swig of his whiskey and his lips drew back from his teeth with the taste. 'It does my head in. She should have left him years ago. Sheila used to be such a cracker of a woman, and now she looks much older than her years.' He put down his glass, picked up his fags and offered one to Jamie. 'Sorry, kid, ignore me. I always spout a lot of shit when I'm pissed.'

'It's OK, I hate him—I always have. As soon as I turn sixteen in a couple of weeks, I'm off. I'm not staying around here to rot like them. I just wish that she would come to her senses and leave him, get herself a life.'

'Aye but your mam's not like that Jamie she'll stay with him till closing time. He has a hold over her and she's too weak to let go.'

Although Jamie had known Ricky's father all her life, she had never really taken a good look at him, and the more time she spent in front of him the more his face reminded her of someone, not Ricky, as he was the image of his mother but someone else.

As Michael came into the kitchen for one last attempt to take Jamie home, it clicked. Everything about him, the same eyes, the same colour hair and skin, even his voice had similarities. It was all making sense to Jamie now as to why her father hated the Webster's so much. It was because of Michael. Her father had always picked on him and she never knew why. She knew that her mam had some big secret, as she had almost told Jamie a few times when she had been defending her father after his violent outbursts. She had always said that she was the real problem in the relationship and shouldn't have behaved the way she did when he was away. Jamie had thought that this might have been the case, as her father had also shouted out in his rage that Michael wasn't his son, and that Sheila should have got rid of him when she had the chance. But she had never thought of Ricky's father being in the equation. She may be wrong, she thought, but there were some striking similarities the more she studied them both.

'Bout ye Michael? Come and sit with us fella, your sister is keeping me company. Can I get you some grub or a drink?'

'No thanks, Mr Webster, I'll just take Jamie home if I can.'

Tom Webster rose to his feet and motioned for Jamie to hug him.

'Come here, wee lass. You can still come over anytime you want to—and you Michael, we may not be the best company at the moment, but if you need us we're here for you both. Ricky thought a lot of the two of you, he used to tell me how you and he were like soul mates Jamie.'

As they approached the front door, he handed Jamie a box.

'I'd like you to have his records, Jamie—he would have wanted that. Maybe you could come by next week and pick up the rest? I haven't had the heart to go in his room yet. This lot were his favourites, he was playing them—that day.'

Jamie nodded her reply and as the tears welled up in her eyes, Michael said their goodbyes and took Jamie home.

For two weeks she stayed in her bedroom mourning her only true friend. She played his records continuously with only her guitar for company. There were moments when she thought that she could smell him: a mixture of old BO, Lynx and dope would fill the room. She had talked to no one, not even her brother, and no one had bothered to come knocking to find out if she was OK.

When her grief was finally manageable, she attempted a few times to sit outside Heather's house, hoping to get an explanation as to why she hadn't been in contact. She couldn't call her on the phone in case her father still had a ban on them having anything to do with each other. Her father Jimmy would never forget his meeting with Mr Gardner, and she was still getting slapped about by him over it. Her school days had come to an end, so there were no opportunities for them both to be in the same place at the same time. She felt alone. Even Abi, whom she thought of as a new friend, had deserted her and refused to see her. She eventually gave up when she saw Heather from a distance getting into her dad's car with a suitcase. There was no point in calling after her, as she knew her father would be taking her to start a new college life. She would have to accept that it was over and carve out some sort of life for herself.

She had left school with no qualifications as she didn't sit any exams. Her father had told her she had to get a job sharpish as he wasn't going to be giving her any handouts, so she went to the careers office to find out if there were any jobs going.

The careers adviser sat at the desk in her polyester two-piece banging the side of the computer monitor to make it work faster for her. She had warned Jamie about the growing unemployment lines and tried to get her to join a youth training scheme at the supermarket.

'The thing is, Miss Taylor, you have to take what you can get these days as all the best jobs are taken by those with qualifications, and you don't have any do you?' She spoke under her breath as she scrolled through the pages. 'No—that's no good—you're too, shall we say tomboyish to work as a salon apprentice so YTS. shelf stacker is all I can offer you I'm afraid.'

Jamie seemed half interested. It was either that or the first job that she had turned down of working on a farm, and she didn't feel like getting up at the crack of dawn to tend to sheep.

'Well? come on girl I haven't got all day am I putting your name forward or what?

She eventually agreed and everything seemed to be going well until they talked about the uniform, she would have to wear; a red and grey striped dress and sensible shoes. This was something Jamie had no intention of even contemplating. She had stifled her identity for all her school life, so there was no way she was going back to that.

'Look—wait, surely it will be OK if I wear trousers?'

When confronted with the question, the careers adviser replied with a scornful face, 'the men wear the trousers, and the women have to look their best to be pleasing on the eye for the customers.'

'So much for Girl Power,' she said, and politely declined.

When she told her father that she wasn't taking any fucking job in a skanky supermarket, he slapped her from one side of the kitchen to the other. That was the last time he would ever get the chance to hit her, she thought. She packed up what little belongings she had and waited until he fell asleep to make her next move.

If she was going to slum it in Cardiff, she needed money, and her dad had won a hundred pounds on the horses.

As he slept, lazing in his chair with his hand down his pants, his wallet had slid halfway out of his pocket. Jamie got down on her knees by the side of the chair and gently pulled it the rest of the way out. As she took the hundred pound out and shoved it into her pocket, she noticed a photo of her as a baby in her dad's arms. He was in his Welsh Guards uniform, standing outside the QE2. Her mother always said that he had been a good soldier and didn't deserve the burns he received aboard the Sir Galahad in the Falklands. It had been that solitary moment that his personality had changed forever.

Jamie paused before putting his wallet back and thought how things may have been different if he hadn't got on board. The cut on her lip that she had received from him earlier broke open when she wiped away the single tear that had fallen for him. It was then that she remembered the bastard he had become.

She got back on the floor and nuzzled the wallet back into his pocket. He woke with a jump and moved over in his chair. She put her head down and kept as still as stone, waiting without breathing for him to drop back off to sleep. It took ten minutes before she felt safe enough to move and had pins and needles in her legs as she crawled through the doorway without looking back. She filled her rucksack with beer and the sandwiches that Sheila had made for his tea before she went for a lie down herself. There was no going back now, even if she wanted to. She would never get that money back in his pocket, and if she were here when he found out that it was missing, he would kill her for sure.

On her way out, she could hear the clanking of the beer bottles knocking together and hoped to god that he didn't hear it. She opened the front door and gently closed it behind her. She was out. Now all she had to do was get on the bus and she would be free.

She had been waiting in the rain for ten-minutes so figured that one was due any minute now. She stared at the corner, willing it to come. The bus stop wasn't that far from the house, and she could see the outline of what looked like her father coming up the road. As she concentrated on the figure to make sure she wasn't imagining things, the bus drove past him and lit up his shadow. It was him. As soon as he noticed her, he started to run, but the bus got there first. As she sat down, she gave him the finger through the window as he banged the back of the bus with a hard thump.

Chapter 11

2009 cont.

As her coffee took hold the summer of 96' became a distant memory for Jamie, some good times and some she prayed that one day she would have the courage to forget.

She had often thought about Ricky and what would have become of him if he hadn't had his young life taken away from him so tragically. With all the changes in technology in such a small space of time, she wondered what he would have thought of all these mass music storage systems of today. She had hundreds of records given to her by Tom Webster and they were all stored in boxes at the club just in case she wanted to dig them out to reminisce, of which she did often. The sound of a needle scratching around the surface compared to the crystal silence of a CD was a sad loss of nostalgia, she thought.

His record collection helped her to carve out her own future pathway and made her who she was today. She was grateful for that as a respected nightclub owner, DJ, and singer. When she performed at weekends, her sets contained all the old songs that made her and Ricky's youth so memorable, and every time she sang it took her back to the council estate; running around with Ricky and trying not to get caught.

Even now years later she felt his presence watching over her with every new mix she saved to a memory stick. That part of technology Ricky would have relished, as it would have suited his laid-back lifestyle not carrying heavy record boxes around anymore. She figured he would have hated all the social networks though, with everybody knowing everyone else's business and nowhere to hide your secrets. The tracking systems in place now; knowing where you are at any given time wouldn't have helped his cheeky ways much either.

She was straddling the line of the law now, as most of her troubles were self-inflicted or of the emotional kind. She left all her dodgy dealings on the council estate the day she left and hadn't returned since.

Accepting a friend request from Heather would bring the past back to life, and she wasn't sure that she wanted to go there. Her life was so different now. She wasn't that scared little sixteen-year-old running from her father's belt-straps anymore. She was lucky enough to have had the pleasure of many women in her twenty-nine-years, but very few had broken down her barriers to touch any part of her heart the way her first love did. This was the real reason she had doubts about accepting the friend request. She knew that if she had felt this much of an attraction in her teenage years, there was no telling how the woman in her would react.

Ignoring the urge to respond straight away, she scanned over her emails for distraction. This wasn't a decision to be made lightly, and she needed the shock to sink in first. *Viagra at rock-bottom prices,* was the first to be displayed then her very own favourite: *Have you had an accident recently that wasn't your fault?* Everyone was out to make a quick buck on suing each other, it seemed. You couldn't even bump into someone with your supermarket trolley without them screaming whiplash and compensation, she thought. Whatever happened to robbing someone the good old-fashioned way by breaking into their house or stealing their car? Everything was done by identity theft or online scamming these days.

The next email was to be more lucrative as it was from the estate agents. She had been looking for a house to buy that was far enough from the centre but not total suburbia. No luck this time: the property the estate agent had flagged up for her was in a quiet neighbourhood full of the 2.4 children brigade. She would stick out like a rat among a box of mice, she thought.

Living and working at Jewel's had its share of good and bad points, but living with her brother Michael made her feel like she was living in a goldfish bowl. People were always staying over, and she felt as if she had no privacy. She had taken to staying over random girl's houses for days at a time just for the peace, away from his entourage. This always gave the wrong impression of commitment to whoever she was with, and she didn't want to make any empty promises. Most of the girls she went home with were from a late-night dive, or just a pickup from a bar after work, but never her own. Either way, she would have been paralytic at the time and wouldn't have been able to pick them out of a line up the next day.

Living with her brother had started as a temporary arrangement while he was working for her at the club. She hadn't intended it to be more than a few weeks. But the more famous he became, the more her big sister instincts kicked in and she felt it safer to keep an eye on him.

Michael's alter ego was supposed to be short-lived. It started as a publicity stunt, and a good reason to shave off his George Michael stubble and keep him out of trouble. Dressed in a silver sequined jumpsuit with pinch-toe sling-backs, he was employed to walk the High Street handing out flyers to promote the club. When the promotion ended, he had got so good at the role it became a regular thing, and with a little help from his flamboyant friends the quick-witted banter drag queen, 'Tilly Moans' was born.

In his mind, it was also a good way to put two fingers up to his father, and the more clubs he appeared at, the more popular he became, especially with the older men who would buy him anything he asked for. He used this to his own advantage. In his eyes they were sad perverted old bastards that deserved all they got, so sharing expensive cruises with them and weekends away in Paris and Rome were always taken advantage of.

The rest of the men were average Joes, playing it straight in the sober world, and releasing their inner Mariah in private. If Michael were ever to talk to them as himself, they would feign ignorance, deny all knowledge of who he was and dismiss him with disgust. It amazed Michael how these men could go home to their wives and kids and act as if everything were normal. If being tossed off by a bloke in a dress was normal then carry on, he would say, but as they were paying him, he would never reveal their secrets and was only too happy to oblige.

Michael craved the attention. He needed to erase the feeling of loneliness that he had suffered throughout his childhood. But behind the size ten four-inch heels he was still that scrawny little kid locked in a shed, only this time it was *him* keeping the real Michael inside. No matter how many people he surrounded himself with, he still felt alone.

The friend request was still flashing away at her from the top of the screen. The hard exterior she now showed to the world made it almost impossible for her to deal with the emotions she had stirred inside her. With her curiosity getting the better of her she clicked on

Heather's profile to get an idea of who the adult Heather had become but unlucky for her there were restrictions in place stopping any photos or statuses being seen. Would it really hurt to respond to the request? It was not as if they had to meet up or anything, she thought. She knew she was kidding herself. The thought of seeing her again made every inch of her body contract. She clicked accept, then typed a message to accompany the response. All the feelings of the past came back to her like a slap in the face as she typed.

I want to ask how you're doing after all this time, but it doesn't sound enough. I often think about our time together and racked my brain for an explanation as to why you kept your distance on the day of the funeral, but hey, the past is in the past and I know you must have had your reasons. Watching you from the bridge on the day you left for college still feels like yesterday. I wanted to shout over to you, but at the time my heart wouldn't let me. I think I knew then that I would never see you again.

Why I'm telling you this now, I don't know lol. Time moves on and so did we.

Anyway, I hope life has been kind to you and that you're happy. Still can't believe I'm typing this to you—and to say that it shocked me to see this friend request would be an understatement. I have buried that part of my life away so deep that sometimes I think I was born the day I left the estate at sixteen.

Can't believe it's you...

She pressed send, and as soon as she did, she wanted to cancel it. Today's Jamie wasn't the type to be dwelling in the past, but there was no going back now. She closed the laptop lid down firmly as if she were shutting the door on the past and dragged her thoughts back to the present.

* * *

It was an extra busy Saturday night in Cardiff, and Jewels was no exception. Not only were people out celebrating for Valentines Day, but Wales had beaten England at rugby. The music was screaming its way out of the building, calling out to the passing trade along the High street. It clashed with the voices of the fans singing 'Delilah' by Tom Jones at the top of their lungs. Their smudged red faces of what once were Welsh flags painted on skin had now mixed with sweat and beer as they marched past. Others were queueing up outside and shuffling their way ahead, but the gangs of drunken rugby boys were eventually turned away, while the bouncers chose to let the regulars and the ladies that were easier on the eye in first.

The nightclub was filled with hen party's and gay men hitting it hard on the dance floor. The poolroom was dominated by diesel dykes in an army of red, hogging the pool tables as if their life depended on it. Half-filled beer bottles and rugby mementoes filled the tables while leather and denim jackets lay strewn over chairs waiting for their owners to vacate the dance floor. No one seemed to care about how intimate they were with each other, and the dark shadows and corners held their own secrets.

Up in the DJ booth, Jamie had finished her set for the night and was handing over to the next DJ. The perks of being the boss meant she could finish at her own time and always had a stand-in DJ on call to take over. With her back leaning over the barrier below, Sam, Jamie's long-suffering friend, had been waiting for over an hour for Jamie to finish. The Gel in her Mohawk had melted with the heat from the lights and tiny beads of sweat ran down her face causing her piercings to sting. She waved her arms frantically to get Jamie's attention and shouted up to her hoping she'd be heard over the music 'Jamie, it's nearly 11 o'clock are we going to this house party or what?'

Jamie signalled to Sam that she was watching the dance floor. She had noticed a young girl trying not so discreetly to sell drugs to a couple of newcomers. This was something you were never going to fully control in a nightclub, but she hated it when a so-called dealer made it so obvious. The girl only looked about nineteen and hadn't a clue what she was doing.

Jamie squeezed herself down the winding steps from the DJ booth to put an end to what she had witnessed; she had designed the steps that way for less traffic. In other venues she had played, there was always some idiot that would insist they could do a better job and not leave you alone trying to push sliders and press buttons. But that wasn't the worst distraction. She would also have a constant string of women and men chatting her up whilst spilling their drinks over her equipment. With a spiral staircase and not a lot of room to move, this meant she only had the girls she wanted in her tiny space, and that made life a lot easier. She pushed herself through the crowd and passed Sam on the way. 'I'll be two minutes, mate. I just need to deal with blondie on the dance floor and her bags of snow.'

Sam looked over to who Jamie was about to confront, then shook her head in disbelief. She signalled for Jamie to come back. She figured that Jamie only had one brain cell to use when she was pissed and that controlled the contents of her pants, so she knew she had forgotten. 'Hey mate, shell leave when we do it's her fucking party remember.'

Jamie looked a little puzzled, then jumped to the wrong conclusion as usual. 'For fuck's sake, Sam, who is she? You know I have to be careful of the undercover pigs in here after the raid on 'The Moonraker.' They are talking about closing it down after their last lock in got out of hand. Dai the owner is going out of his mind.'

Sam scoffed at the suggestion her friend had landed on her. 'Woh, steady girl—it's got nothing to do with me. She's your little American friend, not mine.'

A disbelieving Jamie squinted her eyes to get a better look.

'I guess you can't remember fucking her last night in the toilets of that pizza place either then. I told you she was a bit of a head case, but you insisted her accent made you wet and she was too fit not to fuck. You kept going on about this house party, and how you were gonna meet some up-and-coming artists to book in the club.'

Jamie tried to recall the few memories she had from the night before as they made their way to the bar. She climbed underneath the hatch and poured her mate a whiskey.

'Shit Sam, what would I do without you and your amazing drunken memory. I don't know how you do it. You were as wrecked as me last night and to be completely honest, I'd forgotten what she looked like. You don't have her name floating around in that head of yours by any chance, do you?'

'You're gonna get yourself into so much shit one day, Jay—I think it was Zoe or something similar.'

'Zoe, yeah, that's actually triggering something in my head. I think she said she worked for Storm Radio.' Jamie seemed excited at her recollection.

'Trust you to remember that and not her name or what she looked like.'

Jamie gave her a sideways smile, quickly necked half a bottle of Jack and shivered with the taste. 'I've gotta start taking more water with it, Sammy—but not tonight, hey.'

Sam went outside to flag a taxi down, and Jamie grabbed hold of the girl on the dancefloor. 'Next time ask me before you get your sweets out for sale in my club blondie OK.' The girl gave a mischievous smile and flung her arms around Jamie's neck, raising her short white skirt in the process. As it did, the ultraviolet light kicked in to reveal all that lay beneath.

'Would you like me to get my candy out for you now Jamie, I know how you like to lick, and for your information, I wasn't selling—I was buying so get off my case.'

Sam had managed to hail a taxi so no time for Jamie to be dealing with this now. She fed the information to the bouncers to sort out and then left.

After being in this situation so many times before Sam knew the drill, she jumped in the front seat to let the two girls fall into the back. The taxi driver pulled off as Jamie pushed the dividing window between them shut. Jamie pulled Zoe closer and had the girl sit astride her. Whilst passionately kissing Zoe's neck, Jamie slid her hand between her thighs and gently stroked the outside of her panties. She could feel the wetness of her enjoyment already. She pushed the crotch to one side for easy access and entered her with one, then two fingers. Her pulse was beating hard and Jamie could feel the muscles inside her tightening around them. This aroused Jamie even more, and she could feel herself in need of stimulation. She undid her own jeans and rubbed herself hard with her other hand in time with the pounding of Zoe.

As the windows steamed up, the groans coming from them both were embarrassing Sam, so she asked the taxi driver to turn his music up to drown them out. Conveniently though the overweight bald lump of a man misheard and turned it off instead. This annoyed the hell out of Sam, and she suggested politely that he should pay more attention to the road and not what was going on in the back.

The taxi was swerving out of control as the smell of sex and leather filled the small, unassuming space. Jamie had Zoe close to climax and the taxi driver could hear the tension. Excited, he pulled away at his own trousers that had suddenly shrunk tight around his crotch as he bolted upright in his seat, squinting and squirming to get a better look. He was out of luck—little was left of their modesty, safely hidden away in the shadows. He would have to be content with just the audio commentary as he groped at himself over the sound of Zoe's head pounding on the roof of the taxi. The louder she screamed, the more the sweat poured off his jowls and circled his shirt collar. As she let out her last screams in orgasm, the taxi driver came close to exploding with her and grabbed the steering wheel hard with one hand.

When they finished, Zoe climbed back into her seat, adjusted her dress and lit up a fag. Her face glistened in the flame's light and as she exhaled, she saw the taxi driver scowling at her in the mirror. As soon as he could take his hand off the wheel, he started banging on the divider window.

'There's a non-smoking sign right in front of you, can't you read? Now put it out.'

Jamie grabbed the dividing window and caught the taxi driver's hand in it as she forced it open.

'You must be joking, right? So, it's alright to fuck in your taxi mate but not for her to smoke. I could see you in the mirror licking your lips. Your eyes were darting everywhere trying to get a better look at the floor show, you weren't complaining then.'

'Just tell the tart to put it out or get out of my fucking car. Is that clear enough for you?'

Zoe leaned over and took a drag on the fag, then blew it directly at him through the divider window before laying her views on him. 'I bet you'd like a good blow, you fat greasy perv.'

The taxi swerved to a parking position, throwing the girls to the floor with the impact. The driver got out and opened Jamie's door. Without hesitation, he pulled Jamie out of the car and on to the ground, kicking her in the process.

'No one speaks to me like that now get your slag and fuck off—go on.'

As the taxi driver went to open the other two doors, Jamie rose to her feet and followed him. He laughed out loud as she walked towards him with her fists clenched.

'If you're gonna act like a geezer, then you take it like one. Fucking dykes, you think you're so invincible. Come on—throw one punch at me and I'll have your arse for assault.'

Sam and Zoe got out of the car and stood behind him. Before Sam could stop her, Zoe hit him on the back of his head with the heel of her shoe. He dropped clean to the floor, banging his head hard on the tarmac as he fell.

Sam was never one for altercations, and she immediately jumped to her own conclusion.

'What the fuck, he's not moving—she's killed him.' Not wanting to confirm her suspicions, she dropped to her knees and with a newfound strength managed to turn him over. There was a trickle of blood where the floor had come up to meet him, but nothing that looked too serious. 'He's still breathing, at least, but I don't think we should be here when he wakes up. Let's leg it now before things really get out of hand.'

'Not yet. I think I've left my phone in the car.' Zoe's phone was tucked neatly inside her handbag and she knew it. This was just a ploy to get what she wanted. She knew exactly what she was doing as she climbed into the front of the taxi and luckily for her *Fat Boy* had left the takings box open. Unknowing to Jamie and Sam, she took every penny and shoved it everywhere she could fit among her person. 'That will teach the perverted fuck,' she whispered under her breath.

Jamie used the car to steady herself on. The kicks had taken her breath away for a moment, but she could walk.

Clutching her stomach, she gave the taxi driver a recip-rocated kick which nearly knocked her off her feet. As she gained her balance, Sam caught sight of him moving and shouted over to them.

'Let's leg it, quick he's opening his eyes.'

As the girls fled, the guy ambled to his feet and hold-ing his head he strained to see which way they went. He caught sight of them heading towards the church at the bottom of Mill Street and shuffled himself back into his taxi.

He fumbled around with his keys to start the engine. Then, as he put the car into gear, he noticed the empty takings box. After slamming his fist on the dashboard, he slammed his foot down on the accelerator and fol-lowed in angered pursuit.

As they got to the Church, the perimeter fence that surrounded it was never-ending and they hacked their way through the stinging bushes, desperately looking for a way in. Eventually making it to the gate, they faced a six-inch padlock. No one was getting in there. The fence was not the easiest to climb either, and the three of them desperately tried to scale it, falling back down with every clumsy step.

They heard the taxi come to a screeching halt behind them and scarpered with all the energy they had left to make it to the side gate. This time they were in luck. The bars on the gate had been forced apart previously, and they eased themselves between the rusted iron. Jamie pushed Zoe through first and then squeezed through herself. Sam knew that there was no way she would fit her beer gut through, but tried anyway. In the distance, they could hear the out of breath wheezes coming from the driver. His heavy-footed amble was getting closer, and the girls panicked.

'Sam, there's no use trying to mate it was hard enough for me to fit through.' She pointed over to the path behind the houses opposite, 'Make a run for it down there and I'll make sure he sees us behind here. It was nothing to do with you, anyway. It's us he'll be gunning for. There's no way he'll get in here the fat bastard he's eaten way too many pies.'

Sam disappeared just as the taxi driver spotted them, and as they had expected, he made his way straight to the gate. Jamie grabbed Zoe's arm and pulled her backwards out of the bushes. They weaved their way through the headstones, searching for the other side of the cemetery to find a way out. They hadn't noticed how scary the old place looked at night until they stopped in the middle, desperately trying to get their bearings to where the other exit was hiding.

As soon as they found it, they faced another chunky padlock. This time was not so hard, though. There was a branchy tree next to the railings, and they climbed up halfway before hurling themselves over the top to freedom. Jamie didn't want to spend another minute in the cemetery. It kept them safe from an irate taxi driver for a while, but this was not the most inviting place to be after midnight, she thought.

Zoe scrambled around on the grass, picking up the contents of her bag that had fallen out when she fell. It was full of pound coins and scrunched up fivers amongst bits of make-up and a single bag of snow. They made their way across the fields and finally reached the top of Maidstone Hill.

'So where is this party then? It feels like we've been walking around in circles, and I know I've seen that pile of dog shit before.' It was just underneath the 'Vote for us' conservative poster on the side of a bus shelter. They had been banging on about family values and about how the family set up from years ago was a thing of the past. Jamie wasn't really into politics but knew what she knew. It was in the right place, she thought, and looked like the dog had purposely placed it there.

They had left the graveyard half an hour back and could still see it in the distance from the top of the hill, so Jamie knew that they must have doubled back some-where along the line. Zoe sat herself down on the bench inside the shelter and lit up another fag. Jamie was glad of the break from walking too and perched herself along-side her. Zoe took one look at Jamie, then held her head down in shame as she nervously came clean.

'I have a bit of a confession to make about the party—it's not happening. I had a text in the club to say that they cancelled it. If you hadn't jumped me in the cab, I would have told you sooner.'

'So why not tell me about it half an hour ago before we climbed this fucking hill,' she choked? Jamie was still a bit sore from the kicks off the taxi driver, so really didn't need the extra exercise. Zoe had become a lot more trouble than she was worth.

'I thought I'd surprise you. I live up here. We could spend some time together and get to know each other a little better.' Zoe hoped that Jamie had believed her. She didn't want to seem desperate and just wanted to impress. She had only been in the UK a couple of months and was staying at a relative's house. This was the first time that she had wanted to take someone back. All she had to do now was convince Jamie that the house she would take her to belonged to her. Another white lie wouldn't hurt, she thought. She had the house to herself this weekend, so she knew they would be alone. She also needed the company of a new friend desperately, and who better than her.

'What you really mean to say is that you've been lying to me all this time. There never was a house party—was there?' Jamie hated being lied to by anyone and wouldn't take it from someone she hardly knew. 'Why lie to me? There was no need for that—you're a beautiful girl, Zoe, you didn't need to trick me.'

'OK—OK, don't get angry with me—yes, you're right. There never was a party. I just wanted to spend some time with you. I knew if I had just asked you to take me out you would have pushed me aside like I've seen you do to others. Please don't be angry with me.'

Zoe looked relieved that she had finally admitted her little white lie. When she saw Jamie the night before, she knew that unless she had a reason to approach her, Jamie wouldn't have given her the time of day.

She had seen her singing in the club loads of times and had tried to make eye contact, but she had never noticed her back. She had fed her the lie about the party to get her attention and was all she could come up with in such a short space of time. Zoe had told Jamie that there would be a lot of influential people at the party that would promote her club, and as she worked for the local radio station, she had contacts of celebrities that she could get to appear at a fraction of the cost. Jamie fell for the bait and had spent half the previous night listening to her stories of which she now knew were all in her head.

Zoe was in awe and a little flattered that Jamie had remembered about the party, but as she hadn't followed the rest of the details through, she knew that eventually, she would have to cover up her story with another lie. It was a good job that Sam was no longer with them as Zoe wanted Jamie all to herself and she hadn't planned on Jamie bringing someone.

'What the fuck—so why are we here—wherever here is?'

Jamie looked around and remembered that this was the area that the estate agent had sent her an email about. She had completely struck it off her list because of the type of people who lived there. It was full of families and 4x4s in a suburban neighbourhood and not the type of place that a house party as she suggested would have been taking place.

Zoe's plan had fallen apart. She had never been that good at lying and stumbled over her words. She knew deep down that she wouldn't get away with it, but felt it was worth a try. Jamie held no bad feelings towards her and walked an embarrassed Zoe home. They both knew that there was no reason to meet up again and accepted it as so.

Chapter 12

Every Sunday Jewels would hold an open mic night in the lounge bar. Jamie would always open the evening with a few firm favourites on guitar and close the evening in the same way. In between, you would have South Wales' finest buskers getting up and strutting their stuff, hoping to collect some fans along the way.

Tuning up her guitar with the band had taken a little more time than usual, and the bar was filling up before her eyes. Even though it was now eight in the evening, she still had had little sleep from the night before. When she finally made it home it was nearly daylight, but she still rang Sam to check if she'd got home OK before going to bed herself. An hour later she was still on the phone with a bottle of Jack telling Sam all of Zoe's crazy antics. Sam had found it hilarious that someone so young could con Jamie with *her* reputation. She had finally got to sleep for an hour only to be woken by the cleaners in the club with their buffing machines and deep clean Sunday routine.

She struggled her way through the first set and was glad that there were a few acts lined up to perform, relieving her of the pressure. She spent the time downing a few hairs of the dog mixed with Red-Bull. This gave her the energy boost she needed, and she was now back to herself, bouncing all over the stage. Jamie would always finish with a slow song: an emotional tear-jerker to melt the hearts of her mostly female audience. Tonight was no different, and she was glad to finish to grateful applause.

As they lifted the stage lights, the band began packing up. Joely, the bass guitarist, pulled Jamie to one side.

'Looks like you have an admirer there, Jamie, in the grey flannel suit at the bottom of the bar. She hasn't taken her eyes off you all night.' While winding her guitar lead around her arm she nodded as to where she was sitting, and the woman gave Jamie a knowing wave 'I think I'll leave you to it—looks like you're in for another long night boss.'

After most of the crowd had gone, and the barmaids had finished cleaning the tables, Jamie left the stage via the back entrance to avoid direct eye contact with the woman. As she walked closer to the bar, she could feel the woman's eyes still staring at her. Jamie pulled up a stool at the other end of the bar and sat down. It was then that she noticed.

'Hey Jamie, long time no see.'

It was Heather. Her voice was unmistakable. Jamie moved down the bar just to check she wasn't hearing things and as she got closer, she could see the shine of her beautiful green eyes and heart-shaped smile, a little older but as stunning as ever.

'Well, are you gonna give your old friend a hug or have I come all this way for nothing?'

As Jamie held Heather, it felt as if she could close her eyes and reopen them in 1996, standing by the bridge and not wanting the summer to end. Even the smell of her hair was the same. The only difference now was they were both grown women and a lot of water had passed under their bridge.

Jamie was oblivious to Heather knowing that she had cheated on her back then and although she had cheated on many women with no regrets in her older years, she had always deeply regretted this one.

'Wow—I can't believe it's you. This may sound crazy, but I have always wondered how it would feel if we ever met up again, with us being older.'

As soon as she heard herself say the words, Jamie tried to change the subject, protecting herself from letting Heather know that she still thought about her after all this time. This was not the same Jamie from years ago. This was a confident young woman that could enjoy almost any woman she wanted too. There were too many unanswered questions from the past for them to form any type of relationship that involved trust, friendship or otherwise. Heather noticed the signs of panic in

Jamie's voice and tried to reassure her old friend of her intentions.

'Jamie, I'm not here to rake up old feelings I just thought it would be nice to see each other again—as friends, maybe. My life has changed dramatically from how it was back then, and I can see that yours has too. We were too young to have accepted what we went through in such a short space of time, and it took me years to get those images out of my head from that time with poor Ricky.'

Jamie accepted this. Heather was talking sense. It was mainly the shock of being in her company after all this time that was causing an effect on Jamie. She poured them both a drink and they reminisced for a while. Not letting the other know what they were really thinking.

As the alcohol took hold, the conversation turned tense and needy. They both tried to convince each other that they were not the same hapless teenagers trying to take on the world and losing. Neither of the women had any intention of giving themselves into the past. They both had different ideas of what that relationship meant to them, especially Heather. The way Jamie treated her back then, sleeping with her best friend was unforgivable and yet the more she watched Jamie talk, the more she wanted her even now. It surprised her and scared her at the same time.

'I knew you would make something of yourself, you've always had the determination and fight in you.' Heather looked around at the décor. Black and white prints of lesbian icons graced the walls of dark purple. They designed it to house little private nooks in corners, so couples could chill together. 'This place is amazing I had no idea you were such a performer.'

'Neither did I—I just seemed to fall into it. When I left school, things were not working for me at all. It was easier to move away than to work things out. I took most of my stuff and stole a hundred pounds out of my dad's horse winnings and headed for the city. I had nowhere to stay and slept rough for the first week. That was when I met Kay. She was busking around the streets with her guitar and had made enough money to pay for a bedsit. She taught me a few songs, and we were a good team. Singing seemed to come naturally to me, and we were getting quite a fan base. Eventually, we moved out of the bedsit and got ourselves a flat. We weren't a couple or anything as she was very much into men, but we spent a few drunken nights together and that seemed to suit us fine. She's married now with a couple of kids I still see her sometimes pushing a pram around.' Jamie moved to the other side of the bar and tidied up the drip-trays. 'It was her husband I had this place off. We ran it together for a year, then I bought him out. When he first had it, it was used as a recording studio and that is how we all met. We would hire a studio for a couple of hours and record demos to take around the pubs. We gained quite a few gigs that way. But with technology moving on the way it did, more people were using computer software for demo's, so the money wasn't in it. It already had a small bar attached to it upstairs, so I convinced them it could work great as a club—the rest is history. How about you? Has your life turned out the way you wanted it too?'

Heather's body language said it all. She seemed uncomfortable with the question and tried to avoid an answer.

'Sometimes I think it did, and then other days I find myself looking for something else, a better alternative to my everyday lifestyle.' Heather reached for Jamie's hand across the bar. 'We were crazy back then and even though I thought I had made the right decision, I'm looking at you now and wondering if I did.'

There was no mistaking that the passion they had for each other was still there. The conversation seemed to have dropped its pleasantries and had become more intimate yet heated. The sexual chemistry that grew between them was mixing all over again, and Jamie began leading Heather up the stairs to the flat. They both knew the risks they were taking but after ripping each other's clothes off, nothing or no one else seemed to matter.

The sex was hard and heavy. Every time Jamie entered her it was like the power of all the women Jamie had laid with was just a steppingstone to this night. Heather's body although familiar to Jamie had grown into every inch a woman, and she was taking advantage of that. They had shared each other in almost every room of the flat and after reaching orgasm many times they lay naked on the floor of Jamie's bedroom, entangled in a single white sheet.

Jamie felt they could lie there for hours in silence and the rest of the world would stop and wait, but this wasn't the case for Heather. She pulled the sheet from Jamie, stood up and left her naked on the floor.

'There are other things I need to talk to you about Jamie, but not tonight. I must get to work shortly. Is it OK if I take a shower?'

Without waiting for an answer, she grabbed her mobile from her jacket then kissed her once again before heading for the door. Not wanting Heather to leave so soon, Jamie climbed onto her bed and shouted through the ensuite door.

'So, what is it you do that keeps you out as late as this? You never mentioned.'

There was silence for a few seconds, so Jamie assumed that Heather hadn't heard her over the sound of the shower. As she leaned over to the crack in the door to say it again, she saw Heather getting angry with her phone, desperately trying to send a text with her hands a little shaky. Not wanting to give her any more grief, she left the question for another time and lay back on the bed. A little while later Heather came in wrapped in a towel and drying her hair. She rushed about picking up her clothes as Jamie watched in awe of how incredibly beautiful she still was.

'Sorry I took so long—I had soap in my eyes.'

Hopping on one leg to put her trousers on whilst frantically doing up her blouse buttons gave Jamie the feeling that she was in a real hurry and the coldness of it all perturbed her.

'Look Jamie I really have to go but I will be in touch I promise.'

Jamie nodded as Heather threw her jacket around her, then grabbed her keys. She gave her one last kiss before leaving, almost slamming the door behind her.

This left Jamie with doubts. It was good to have seen Heather, but with her leaving so rapidly, she worried if Heather may have regretted their little encounter. Had it left her with an empty promise? Or maybe she did have to work. As she lay on the bed burnt out from the night's antics, her body gave in to a much-needed sleep.

As Jamie opened her eyes, Michael startled her by hovering above.

'Have you seen my mobile anywhere, Sis?'

This freaked Jamie out and she already had her hands up to punch him, as for the first few seconds she didn't realise it was him. When she realised it was him, she wanted to punch him even more. She threw her pillow directly at him and told him to get out while she climbed into last night's clothes.

'For Christ's sake, Michael a good-morning would've been nice!' She rubbed her eyes and made her way to the kitchen, yawning all the way.

'What the fuck went on in here last night, Sis? It looks like a bulldozer has been through the place. I'm glad I stayed out now.'

The flat was upside down and inside out. There were books knocked off shelves, lamps upturned, and the kitchen table had taken such a beating that it was leaning to one side.

Jamie went to the fridge and swigged down some orange juice, then squinted as she inspected the flat loosely. 'I don't quite know myself—it all seems a bit of a blur now. To be honest, I think I may have been played.'

She had this niggling feeling that Heather had just slept with her as *a better alternative to her everyday lifestyle*, as Heather had put it herself. Something with a little danger just to break up a dull marriage maybe, she thought. Her newly arisen brain was making things up as it went along. All she could focus on was the fact that she had left straight after having sex, and in her books that was something you did after you had finished playing with someone. She knew only too well the implications of this.

Michael stopped looking for his beloved phone and went straight to the kitchen 'nothing like a bit of Karma to start the day,' he thought. There was no way he'd let this one go.

'You've—been played! After all this time someone has actually got their own back on you at last.'

'Yes Michael, you could be right, but there's no need to be so callous about it, you're the biggest player of them all. Your acquaintances don't even make one-night stands they are more on the hourly rate. Anyway, this time it's different.'

'God, Jamie, you haven't actually fallen for someone, have you?'

'No—It's not like that. Can you remember Heather from the old days? I accepted a friend request from her, and she turned up at the club. She must have gone through my online profile and found the club from there. I'm probably paranoid, but I felt as if I'd been used as a booty call. We were talking about old times and then we ended up in bed together. I thought everything was going well, but then she left, in quite a hurry.'

'How many times have you done that to someone, Sis? You're just pissed because she did it first. I know you had this big thing going on when we were kids Jame' but that's it—we were kids. Things are different now. You don't know what's going on in her life or she yours. Just take it as a compliment that she wanted to revisit the past.'

'Maybe you're right. I need nothing more than that anyway—you know me always ready to up and leave when there's any sign of commitment.'

As Jamie said the words, she wanted them to be true, but lately, the thought of hitting thirty with no special someone to spend it with was kicking its shoes in the back of her mind.

'Just shake it off Sis, go out tonight and work your magic on some poor unexpected female you will have forgotten all about it by tomorrow. Now where the fuck is my phone? I can't have lost it I have my entire life on there.'

He frantically started flipping cushions and rushing around looking for it.

Jamie had a suggestion, but it didn't involve finding his mobile phone it was more like where he could stick it when he found it.

'Why don't you ring it instead of tearing up the place?'

'I can't ring it I've lost my phone what a stupid thing to say.'

'We do have a landline phone, Michael, or have you forgotten that?'

'Duh—Christ, I'm stupid sometimes.'

He rang his number and was pleased with the outcome. 'Thank fuck for that.'

He reached over Jamie's shoulder and picked up his mobile that was ringing right next to her. She knew it was there but figured as he had so rudely woken her up; she wasn't going to tell him.

'Right, I'm off, I've got a meeting with a very sexy busboy that I've been waiting for and you know what buses are like just when you've been waiting for ages for one, two come along together so watch out Glade Hotel Mamas coming.'

As Michael left and locked the back door of the club, he was met by two police officers.

'Good morning sir, sorry to disturb you but is the licensee around?' The police officer took out his notepad as if to check the text. 'We believe it to be a Miss Jamie Taylor.'

Michael panicked for a second, as he thought that they might have been for him; so, it relieved him when his sister's name was mentioned, in a selfish sort of way. There were a few unsavoury characters that could drop the police a few stories if they needed to about him, as his personal life had a lot of colour.

'Yes, Officer, she's inside. I'm her brother is there anything I can help you with?'

'We need to speak to her directly if that's OK.'

Michael invited them in and told them to wait in the bar while he went to get Jamie. This wasn't the first time she had dealt with the police, as with owning a club it was an unfortunate occurrence.

'Jamie, there are two police officer's downstairs wanting to talk to you, I've left them in the bar. I know it sounds a bit self-absorbed and even though the one is fucking gorgeous is it OK if I get off—you know, busy day and all.'

Jamie knew that Michael would have been no help even if he was to stay. He had a habit of opening his mouth at the wrong time and saying things he shouldn't when it came to the police, so she was glad to see him go.

'I understand Mikey, you go and do exactly what you accused me of doing an hour ago.' He minced his way out of the apartment on purpose for a reaction. Jamie shouted after him as she headed downstairs to the bar. 'Don't forget you're on stage tonight so don't wear yourself out too much will you.'

The police officers stood staring at the liquor lined up at the back of the bar and Jamie felt a hint of fear, hoping that they were all legit and not the ones she had bought at the market.

'Good morning, Miss Taylor. Thanks for taking the time to speak to us again. I'm not sure whether we explained it to you last night, but we are investigating an incident that took place on Saturday evening and we have reason to believe that the people involved were in your club previously. It's the usual routine we need the CCTV footage you may have from outside the front entrance if possible. We know that it may take some time, but if you could drop it to Detective Inspector Williams any time soon that would be a great help.'

This was not an unusual request, and she didn't mind helping. They had a few homophobic idiots that would turn up outside her venue and throw their weight about, so she always kept the cameras running in case it ever got out of hand.

'That's no problem officer I should have it ready for him tomorrow or the next day at the earliest, I'll drop it into the station.'

'That would be great, Miss Taylor. Not sure if she introduced herself properly, but it's the female D.I Williams—as in the one that spoke to you last night—I understand that she had to rush to another case so as you are on our beat anyway, we thought we would let you know.'

At first, Jamie had to think if there was anyone that looked like a police officer in last night, but then it hit her: D.I Williams as in Heather Williams nee Gardner.

Heather, a copper. This couldn't be true. She always seemed so bookish. She would have had her pegged down as a lawyer or an accountant like her dad, but not a copper, she thought.

'Yes, officers—I think I remember now. She wasn't here for very long.'

'We will leave you a card and her mobile number in case you may have any further enquiries. Sorry, it's not an office number Miss Taylor, but she hasn't been in this station long so hasn't been allocated an office yet.'

Jamie accepted the number willingly and showed the officers through the door. The CCTV footage needed to be transferred on to a disc, so she started the recording off to let it run whilst she got her head together.

Chapter 13

Michael had been on stage performing as Tilly Moans for almost an hour with Jamie queueing in his tracks for him. His rendition of the old favourite 'Que Sera Sera' or 'Kiss my Arse' as he had so aptly named it always went down a storm as the crowd sang along with every word. It was the last week of the month, so people were spending their hard-earned money relentlessly at the bar; the alcohol-fuelled atmosphere becoming tense and unruly.

As Michael left the stage for a quick costume change behind the curtain, the crowd started to get restless. The wig he had chosen especially for the last song was too high to get under the stage ceiling lights, so this had him desperately looking for a way to get himself back on before his interval music ran out. He came up with the only logical solution, he would have to go on without it and make a joke of the fact when he got out there. Most of the audience saw the funny side of it except for one weedy little guy from the office party in the front row. They had paid money in advance and booked a table, so wasn't impressed that the drag queen had come on stage just looking like a 'fucking queer,' as he put it. He then decided he would take it upon himself to call Michael an amateur and throw the remainder of his drink over him, glass and all.

The pint glass missed Michael by an inch and Jamie pushed the panic alarm for the bouncers to come immediately to the stage. Before they had a chance to arrive Michael had kicked off his six-inch heels, leapt off the stage and punched the guy clean off his chair. As he did, there was an uproar from the crowd and the embarrassed office nobody was escorted out of the club by the bouncers. When Michael stepped back on to the stage, he made a complete mockery of the incident. The remaining office workers told him how much of a nob the guy was, and that they couldn't wait to tell the rest of their work colleagues what had happened. This was enough for Michael to know, so he left the situation alone. They played out with Tilly singing 'My Way' and when he left the stage, they gave him a standing ovation.

The lights were lifted, and Jamie left for the evening with her usual last song: 'Goodbye' by Alexia. When this was played the audience knew that it was time to leave. They had to down their drinks quickly or the bouncers would take them from them.

With the house lights on and the stage lights not beaming in her eyes anymore, Jamie could see the familiar figure of Heather at the bar, again. This time Jamie saw her as a police officer and not the girl she once knew. As she left the stage, she focused her gaze straight ahead with no eye contact for Heather, and when she arrived, she took the copy of the CCTV footage from below the bar and placed it directly in front of her.

'Thanks for saving me the journey to the station D.I Williams I'm assuming this is what you came in for?'

Heather was feeling a little annoyed that they had exposed her before she'd had a chance to explain. And accepted how Jamie must have been feeling about it all.

'I'm sorry, Jamie. I did plan to tell you straight away, and then when we were getting on so well together, I felt it would have—killed the mood a little.'

'Kill the mood!' she scoffed 'Would you have bothered looking me up—if you hadn't needed something from me?' She reacted to the look on Heather's face. 'Sorry, that was probably a bit harsh, it's just—I felt a right twat when your officers came in this morning. I had no idea you were a copper—it would have been nice to know that's all.'

'Jamie, if I had told you at the start, do you think I would have stood any chance with you taking me seriously? I sent you a friend request long before all of this happened. It's just a coincidence that I would then be working on this case. When I first arrived here, I noticed that a Jamie Taylor was on the club's licensing records and had hoped it had been you. I came down here last week in the day to see if you were around—but it was all shut up. Then I saw the poster on the outside of the club with your face plastered all over it—and I knew it was you. That was when I sent you a friend request.'

This sort of put Jamie's mind at rest. At least she wasn't here just because of work. She leaned over the bar to Heather and whispered in her ear.

'Do you want me to wipe last night's footage of me and you on the stairs off the disc before your team takes a look at it then?'

Heather's eyes widened. She clutched the disc to her chest, not knowing if she was joking or not. She was glad to have secured the recordings before anyone saw them, just in case.

'Don't worry—there's nothing to see. I had you fooled though.' The teasing took the edge off the moment, putting them both at ease. 'When you left so suddenly last night. I didn't know what to think. I figured you may have regretted it or had someone to get home too.'

'I had no choice Jamie they called me back into the station. I had a text to say the case I am working on had moved up a level. I told you it was work. I didn't lie to you—unlike you did to me all those years ago by fucking my best friend.'

Jamie felt herself shrinking. She had hoped that her little secret would never get out. Even after all this time, she felt her palms sweat at the thought of it.

'I hated you so much at that time, Jamie. I wanted to rip your heart out as you did to me. But after everything you had been through with losing your best friend,

I decided staying away was a good enough revenge. Ricky was your world and I just a small part of it you didn't need me adding to your grief. We were young and didn't understand then what we know now. Sometimes things like that just happen, I suppose.'

Jamie could feel herself wanting to defend her actions even though she knew she was in the wrong, 'Things like that wouldn't have happened if you had been truthful in the first place. Abi told me that you were sleeping with Dex. How was I to know that it was all a lie? I know this may seem crazy for me to say it now, but at the time I thought that I was just a pawn in your little game.'

'We were young Jamie with hormones all over the place. Surely, you're not trying to tell me you wouldn't have slept with her anyway, as that would have to be the biggest lie you have told to date. You couldn't spend two minutes on your own with a girl without trying something and by the look of things around here you haven't changed that much either.' Heather walked towards the stage and turned on her foot, 'I saw the way you played the audience the other night you probably have them queueing up around the corner for a night with Jamie Taylor,' she smirked, then returned to her seat. 'I was telling the truth when I said that I hadn't slept with Dex, and I am so glad that I never—things would have been a lot different.'

'Whatever happened to Dexter?'

Heather laughed. She had seen Dexter about five years ago working as a car salesman. He looked about fifty and made the Armani suit he was wearing look like something out of Primark.

'We went to different colleges, so I didn't see him much after our school days. The Thompson brothers are doing well though—one is in Strangeways doing a stretch for murder and the other is a dentist. I think he got a liking for the profession after you knocked his tooth out that time. I used to go the estate quite often when I first passed as a W.P.C. But not since being a D.I—they move you around a lot.'

Jamie had a feeling she knew what was coming next and dreaded the question.

'Do you ever get the chance to see your mother, Jamie? We know all about your father now and what he did to you all. I can't believe I didn't acknowledge it when we were kids. Some copper I would have made back then.'

Jamie had always felt reluctant to talk about her past but felt safe with Heather. 'When I left at sixteen, my father told Michael to tell me that if I ever darkened their door again, he would make my mother pay for it. I tried to see her a few times when Michael was still living at home. He would let me know if it was safe to visit her, then hang around outside the pub keeping watch for my father. Any sign of him returning and he would leg it back home to warn me he was on his way. That was ages ago now—as soon as Michael hit sixteen, he moved up here with me and we haven't looked back since.' She poured herself and Heather a whisky, hoping it would help her continue. 'I know it sounds hard, but nobody knew what he was like. He had this way of manipulating people into thinking they were the ones in the wrong. My mother didn't stand a chance with a thug like that, and still, she always stood up for him. It would have been pointless to even suggest her coming with us as she was loyal to him no matter what—and if that meant losing us kids—then so be it.'

Jamie was feeling a little vulnerable talking so openly about her mother. She felt guilty that they had not tried harder to help her move away from him. Heather had a little information for her that being police she should have kept to herself but took the chance, anyway.

'I remember the police being called to your old address by the guy who lived opposite. He reported that there was a lot of shouting going on and that it sounded like someone was hurt. We broke the door down and saw your mother at the foot of the stairs all battered and bruised.' Jamie shook her head in anger as Heather continued. 'As we entered, he took a swing at one of our officers, so we chucked him in the car and kept him in the cells for the night. He had been heavily drinking, so the swing missed, but it was obvious that he had been hitting your mother as his fists were covered in her blood. Later, when we tried to arrest him for assault, we couldn't. Your mother insisted that she had fallen down the stairs and that he had nothing to do with it. Without proof, and no evidence or statement from your mother, we had to let him go without pressing charges. It made me feel sick at the time. I have seen hundreds of cases like that since, but that being my first has always stuck in my head.'

Jamie felt a lump rise in her throat and coughed to ease it back down.

'This was always the problem, Heather. She defended him over everything, and he knew it. That was a sad thing. He treated her like a rag doll, throwing her around the house, but she wouldn't have it any other way. You can't physically make someone come with you if they don't want to, and if we had kept trying, it would have made it even worse for her.'

Heather could see the effect it was having on Jamie and changed the subject. She made a mental note to do an informal check on her parents, hoping that now they were older things may have calmed down. If this could put Jamie's mind at rest, it was worth a try.

'I could stay over tonight, Jamie—If you'd like me to. I don't have to be at work until the morning. Maybe I could cook breakfast?'

This was new to Jamie. She didn't normally let people stay over long enough to have breakfast, but this time she thought it wouldn't hurt to break the habit. 'Are you sure you won't get called away in the middle of the night, Detective Inspector Williams?'

Heather laughed at the sarcasm but already had a plan in place. She had anticipated Jamie's answer and covered all angles not to be disturbed. 'I've made sure this time, Jamie. They think I'm at least two hundred miles away on a safety course, they will just assume that I stayed over—so if you want me—I'm yours.'

* * *

The next morning Heather sneaked into the station with no questions as to how the course went or any mindless small talk about the hotel she had stayed in. After locking herself away, she checked the records regarding Jamie's parents to see if there were any other callouts to their address for violence. Unfortunately, there had been a regular string of suspected beatings over the years with dates showing up on file right up until Christmas of last year. The same old excuses were given to avoid an arrest, and they had issued the same old advice about domestic violence helplines. She had wished that there had been some good news to report back to Jamie, but it seemed that her parent's situation hadn't improved.

She closed the file down and began the arduous scanning of the CCTV footage, hoping to get a good look at the three suspects for the case she was working on. This was always the most boring part of the job, and after the night she had spent with Jamie, her concentration wasn't at its best.

After forcing her eyes open to watch for an hour, she eventually found her suspects. The outcome wasn't what she had expected. After rewinding and replaying for a good number of times, she discovered that Jamie was one of the girls she was looking for. Worrying that someone else would see the footage, she quickly closed the screen down before snatching the disc from the player. Her first instinct was to throw it away as no one else knew she had it, but the copper inside her knew that she should hold on to it just in case.

Jamie had promised to visit Sam before the mundane trip to the wholesalers. She arrived with takeaway coffees and bagels and as expected Heather's name was the chief topic of conversation. It impressed Sam that Jamie was not only sleeping with a copper but a Detective Inspector. This went against all that the girls stood for in the early days; police were the enemy and not to be trusted. But now they were a little older, it seemed sexy in a crude sort of way. Sam had been seeing someone from the tax office and had thought that bad enough so was willing to accept her best friend's conquest.

As they compared notes on who was in the riskiest relationship, she received a withheld number on her phone, of which she answered reluctantly.

'Hi Jamie, it's Heather. Sorry, I've had to ring you from a pay as you go phone, but they record my calls. I haven't got long, so I'll come right out and say it. The people we were looking to detect on the footage—well, one of them was you. By rights, I should invite you down to the

192 ~ KIM HARRY

station for questioning, but I thought I'd give you the chance to give me your story first. Is it OK if we have a bit of an informal chat?'

Jamie was shocked and sure that this must be a misunderstanding. 'I'm bound to be all over the footage Heather it's my club for Christ's sake.'

'I understand that, but I'm gonna have to ask you some questions about Saturday night—completely off the record. The thing is, the footage shows you and two other people getting into a taxi—the taxi driver claims that you beat and robbed him and as a result suffered a heart attack.'

Jamie signalled for Sam to lean in and listen to the conversation before she bit back at the remark, 'What! no way—that's crazy...'

'Let me finish. They found him at the bottom of Mill Street in the bushes by the church. His box of takings had been stolen, and he had suffered a blow to the head by what seemed to have been the heel of a shoe. We know that he picked you up as he radioed it ahead to the desk. So, who else were you with?' The phone lay silent as Heather waited for an answer. 'Jamie—are you still there? You don't have to tell me anything, but if you want me to help before an official enquiry starts—then I can at least try. It will be a lot harder for me otherwise.'

Jamie couldn't believe what she was hearing. She stole nothing, but she couldn't deny it was her in the taxi. She replayed the incident in her head and suddenly remembered that Zoe went back to the car. It must have been her, she thought, and although she had no intention of naming her, she wouldn't take the wrap for her either. 'OK Heather, that's not how it happened at all—it was sort of self-defence, but I know nothing about any money being taken, I swear!'

She told Heather what had happened from the beginning but wouldn't tell her the names of Sam and Zoe as she wasn't a grass. She hadn't been completely honest about not knowing where they both lived either.

'Well, your version of events differs greatly from the story he is spouting. He said that he had told you to get out of the taxi for smoking and then the three of you pounced on him and hit him across the head. He said that he felt your sole intention was to rob him.'

'That's a load of bollocks he was a horrible pig of a man. He chased us for long enough without worrying about his head, it's not our fault he was too fat to run and gave himself a heart attack!'

All Jamie could think of was losing the license on the club. Any trouble with the law shadowed a vast cloud over your head when renewing your license. She hoped that she could go down the self-defence root as he kicked her first before anyone touched him. Regarding the money going missing, she planned a visit to Zoe to find out exactly what had happened.

Heather told Jamie that she had noted down everything that Jamie had said. This unnerved her a bit, but hopefully, she could trust her.

'I went to see the taxi driver in the hospital this morning and he seemed like a bit of an arsehole, so it doesn't surprise me what you're saying about him. He looked fine. They checked his head over and were happy with it. Just a nasty lump. Trouble is, he is adamant that he wants you brought to justice. So far, the only evidence we have of your involvement is on this recording so—maybe you could say the cameras were off on Saturday and there was no footage for you to copy for the police. They would have to believe you. Not everyone can control whether their cameras are working. I'll get rid of the copy you gave me, and fingers crossed, that will be it.'

Jamie couldn't thank her enough, and Heather seemed genuine.

'Leave it with me and I'll see what I can do before anyone else gets involved.'

As Jamie put the phone down, she had a bout of guilt regarding Sam. Saturday night was supposed to be a bit of fun, and now she had got her best friend involved in her craziness. Sam didn't blame her though; they had been through much worse in the past.

Sam pointed her finger at Jamie, 'I knew that little Yankee tart was up to something. I told you we couldn't trust her. This was all her doing and if anything comes of it, I won't be protecting her. She was the one that hit him, so she will be the one taking the blame if it goes tits up!'

Jamie reassured Sam that she would sort it. All she had to do was reboot her drunken memories and find Zoe, then they would be in the clear.

* * *

As Jamie drove to Maidstone Hill, she was dreading to think of how much trouble she would be in if all this got out. Things looked a lot different in the daylight, and she could barely remember where Zoe's house was. The houses all looked the same, but at least the house that she thought might be hers had a car in the drive. A young girl with a small child answered the door and took her by surprise.

'Hi, I'm not sure if I have the right house but does someone called Zoe live here or would you know where, maybe?'

'Oh—um, it's a yes, you have the right house and no. Hang on, I'll get Sarah to explain—I'm only the child-minder.'

As Sarah walked towards the door Jamie had the feeling that she already knew her, and as she tried to place where in her mind the answer was jolted by the soft tone of her voice.

'Jamie Taylor—I bet you don't remember me, do you?'

Her kind face was unmistakable.

'Wow, Miss Halliwell. Sorry if this sounds a bit out of place, but you have hardly changed at all. I would've thought that you would've looked—older.'

Sarah smiled. 'I was only five years older than you in school, it was my first teaching post. It didn't feel as if I was the teacher for most of it though, I was learning every day the same as you lot. Emma mentioned you were looking for Zoe. What has she done now?'

She showed Jamie into the front room and asked Emma if she could take Molly, Sarah's daughter, upstairs for a little while.

'Is Zoe here? I really need to speak to her.'

'Sorry Jamie, she's gone back to the States she left yesterday. Is there anything I can help you with? She doesn't owe you any money, does she? That seemed to be her favourite pastime whilst she was staying here.' Sarah picked up Molly's toys and threw them into the toy basket. 'She's my late husband's niece and was sent here to give her parents a break, she's always off the rails. I normally don't mind, but this time she seemed a lot different. She's not allowed to drink until she's twenty-one over there, and I think she just lets loose in the UK. I can't say no to them as it's nice for Molly to see her family. You have to take the chance when you can with living so far away it's not that easy to just pop out and visit.'

Her drinking is the least of their worries, she thought. The drugs, the stolen money, even her involvement with

Jamie would be a bit of a shock to any family that didn't expect it.

Jamie pondered on whether to explain anything to her old teacher or to keep quiet. Her only worry was that if Heather couldn't close the case, there would be no confession from Zoe leaving all the blame to fall on Jamie and Sam's shoulders.

'Sorry to hear that you're a widow, Miss Halliwell.'

'It's Sarah Jamie, and yes it was an incredibly sad time for us all. Peter and I had already split up, and he had moved back to America. Molly was only a baby when it happened, she's three now. We both wanted different things out of life, and it showed, he really wasn't cut out for parenthood.' She walked to the living room door and closed it, so her daughter couldn't hear her explanation. 'He died in a car crash; Zoe was in the car with him at the time but came out unmarked I think it affected her more than she let on. She tends to live life on the edge now, not worrying about what people may think. They were cut up on the highway and forced off the road. He didn't stand a chance. Sorry, Jamie, you didn't need to know all that. Sometimes I just drift off whilst talking about it—it helps you know.'

'Don't be sorry. It explains a lot really about Zoe. She seemed pretty mixed up. The thing is, Sarah the police are involved, and I don't know what to say to them.'

Jamie told Sarah what had happened without too much of the explicit details. Zoe's escape back home was probably the best thing that could have happened to her, she thought.

'I can give you her number Jamie if you want to speak to her, but I don't want the police to have it yet if that's OK. Also, I don't think it would be good for Zoe if her family knew that she had been involved with you. I don't mean that in a homophobic way it's just if she hasn't told them about her sexuality it would put her in an awkward position. I can go to the police station and explain what has happened to her if you like and maybe pay back the money that had been stolen. Do you think that would do any good?'

'I think it's gonna take a bit more than that, Sarah. The taxi driver was desperate to have some justice done. He doesn't seem the sort to drop the charges and forget about it. I'll be back in touch when I hear more. It was really good to see you again, even if it was in troubling circumstances.'

'You too Jamie and thanks for not going straight to the police and telling them first.'

She felt a little guilty nodding to that statement as she left out the part about Heather being in the picture.

Jamie needed to see Heather. She wanted to explain what was happening before any more surprises arose. As she walked into the police station, she felt uneasy. Even though she had assumed that the police probably knew nothing about her involvement officially, she still approached the desk sergeant reluctantly.

'Hi, is it possible for me to speak to D.I Williams, please?'

'Hang on, he's just here.' He swivelled around in his chair, then called to a tall, handsome man in his forties. The man shut the filing cabinet that he had been searching through and approached the desk.

'Good afternoon, Miss. I've been told you wanted to see me.'

Jamie looked confused and returned abruptly.

'No—sorry. I asked for D.I Williams. I have been helping her on a case she is working on...'

'That will be Heather—she's only been in the station a few weeks and I forget how complicated it can be with the both of us here. Sorry, the desk sergeant should have asked—she's my wife and we are both D. I's here until I move to a new borough next week. I'll see if she's around.'

Jamie had assumed that Heather was divorced by her reactions given when asked about her marriage. This shocked her a little, and that was not easily done these days as she had slept with many a bored housewife just looking for a night of fun. But this time it felt deceitful: this was her beloved Heather.

'I'm sorry she doesn't seem to be here at the moment, can I leave her a message?

Jamie shook her head and walked away. 'No, it's OK—I have her number—Thanks, anyway.'

As Jamie left the station, she pondered over what she would say to Heather when she spoke to her. There had been no promises made between them and everything had seemed to be just as it was, a casual encounter between old friends. Heather would have to mention it, she thought. There was no reason for her to ask. She padded herself down and checked through her pockets for her mobile to call her, but no luck. She realised that the last place that she had it in her hand was at Sarah's house, so she quickly raced back to Maidstone Hill to retrieve it.

As Jamie got out of her car, she noticed how much of a quiet neighbourhood it was. Most people were probably in work with all the kids in school like it should be. It was nothing like a day on the estate where she grew up. People would be sat outside in their string vests or dirty dressing gowns on a beautiful spring afternoon like this, smoking and downing cans for breakfast. This place looked like a Stepford town in comparison.

As she approached the house, she could see Sarah playing in the garden with her daughter Molly. She was a pretty girl with shiny blond hair, big blue eyes and dimples to melt any heart. Jamie could see how much of a good mother she was, and their type of life was a million miles away to anything she had ever witnessed. She waved to them through the gate.

'Jamie—come on in, just lift the latch.'

The rest of the garden was how she would have imagined it, with everything set up for a three-year-old. A pretty-pink playhouse filled with toys and dolls and a garden swing to match. As Jamie stepped closer, Molly hid behind her mother that was kneeling on the grass.

She kept one eye peeping out now and again, just to make sure she wasn't missing out on anything. Jamie smiled at her playfulness.

'Sorry Sarah, I can see you're busy, but I seem to have left my phone here.'

Sarah tried to stand, but Molly pulled her back to the floor. After a compromise, she finally let her stand but still held on tightly to her leg as she walked. She went into the kitchen and brought out the phone.

'Yes—it's here. I was hoping you would come back and get it. We were just about to have some tea; would you like some?'

Before she could answer Molly left her mother's side, grabbed Jamie's hand and led her to the middle of the garden where a picnic blanket was laid out on the grass dressed with plastic cups and saucers. Half-eaten biscuits had been trodden into the mud amid a line-up of dolls sitting patiently, waiting.

Sarah followed and watched in amazement as her demanding little daughter pulled Jamie to the blanket to have tea with them.

'You can sit next to Ted but don't eat his biscuits or he'll growl at you grrr.'

Sarah sat down at the blanket and pulled her little girl to her lap. 'Now Molly, be nice to our guest or she will think you're a big meanie and won't want to have tea with us.'

Molly stared at Jamie for a short while and tilted her head as if to examine her. Just then she asked the question that Jamie was so familiar with answering.

'Are you a boy Jamie or a girl Jamie?'

Jamie laughed at Molly. She was such a forward little girl and Jamie could see her mother in her. 'I'm a girl, Jamie. Now, where is this tea you promised me? I'm very thirsty.'

Molly reached over to her plastic tea-pot in haste 'OK, OK, I'm going as fast as I can. I'm glad you're a girl Jamie, I don't like boys at my tea-parties.'

Jamie drank down her imaginary tea and then Sarah made them a real cup, which they drank in the kitchen while Molly played in her playhouse.

'She's a beautiful little girl Sarah, she's a credit to you.'

'She's my little star. I don't know where I'd be without her sometimes. I think of what she's been through in her little life, with not having her father around and I could cry.' She blew on her hot tea and took a sip to stop a lump in her throat from taking hold. 'I probably do spoil her too much as I overcompensate sometimes, but I can't help it—I just want her to be happy. I work part-time at the school and she stays with the childminder, but even in that short time, I miss her. Do you have any children, Jamie? Or have you ever thought of having any?'

This question came as a surprise to Jamie. Not that she wasn't maternal, it was just that she hadn't had much of a role model within her own family to ever understand the time and patience it takes to raise a child.

'I've never really thought about it, to be honest, Sarah. My life is totally adult orientated. I hardly see daylight with working most nights.'

'I was like you once. I was so wrapped up in my career and partied hard on weekends. Peter was the same. We enjoyed every spare minute we had. The only reason we got married was that I fell pregnant—my mother's advice being, 'It wouldn't look good for a teacher to have a baby out of wedlock,' she insisted. Then when Molly was born, everything changed. All I could think about was being a good mother. But for Peter it was different, he didn't want to leave his old lifestyle and two weeks after we moved into this house, he left me and went back to the States. It's only rented, but I love it here. It's a good place for Molly to grow up.'

As Molly heard her mother mention her name, she came charging up the garden with her hands full of mud. A worm was wriggling helplessly through her fingers. When she got to Jamie, she held it cupped in her hands. She smirked as she crept slowly towards her. 'Jamie, I have a present for you—shh don't tell Mummy.' She uncurled her fingers and dangled it in front of Jamie's face. 'It's Mr Wormy.'

Jamie ran around the garden, pretending to be scared of the little worm that Molly was so obsessed in chasing her with. Eventually, they both gave up and put him back in his vegetable patch. Molly showed her where a big fat juicy slug was also hiding but she couldn't get a grip on it as in her words 'it was all gooey and covered in snot.'

'Jamie, will you come and play with me and Mummy again? You're funny and you run like a girl.' Molly gave Jamie a huge hug and ran inside to wash her hands.

She promised Molly that she would come and play with her again, and as she left the house that early evening, she couldn't believe how much she had enjoyed just being a kid again. It was a welcome change to all the drama that always seemed to follow her around. It was also refreshing to be talking to someone like Sarah. She felt a little awkward at first, as she could only see her as a teacher, and one that she had a massive schoolgirl crush on. But as the day went on, it became more apparent that she was only five years older than her and no different to any other woman of that age that Jamie knew. She had fallen head over heels for someone though, that beautiful little face had melted her heart. She had never dreamed that looking at life through the eyes of a child could be so rewarding.

Chapter 14

When Jamie got back to the club, Heather was sitting outside in her car waiting for her return. Jamie was still undecided on whether to tell Heather that she had met *her* Mr Williams and let Heather lead the conversation, as they made their way inside.

'I have some surprisingly good news for you, Jamie. When I got to work this morning, I started sifting through some old reports regarding our taxi driver Mr Frank Henshaw and found some interesting stuff.'

Jamie felt humble. 'I appreciate you helping me with this, Heather. I know we haven't seen each other for a lot of years, but I don't make a habit of getting into trouble with the law anymore, honest.'

'We all get tripped up from time-to-time Jamie, even me.' Heather put a reassuring hand on Jamie's shoulder, 'You can't predict how other people will react in a situation like that. Christ knows what would have happened if he had caught up with you. This might have been a totally different investigation and we could have been looking for him for an assault on you—so don't worry about it.'

'Well, the way he dragged me out of that taxi felt like he was used to hitting women, so it wouldn't surprise me if he enjoyed throwing his weight around.'

Heather shook her head in acknowledgement. 'Well, this time he's dug himself into a hole. He thought he could get one over on us and play the victim for the compensation pay-out, it seems. As he's been asking a lot of questions about the procedure. He soon changed his mind when I reminded him about his past though—funny that.' Heather reached into her bag and took out an official-looking document. 'I did a bit of digging and found out he was not as squeaky clean as he made out. It says here that he changed his name to 'Fred Henshaw' back in the eighties, around about the time that he married his second wife Susan. Only thing is, there are no legal documents listed to say that he had divorced his first wife, Mary.' Heather laughed. 'The law doesn't take kindly to bigamists, so being the kind and caring D.I that I am, I thought that I would pay him a little visit at the hospital for a few questions of my own.'

Jamie gave a sigh of relief added with a touch of confusion, 'I can't believe that anyone married him once, let alone twice. I would have loved to have seen his face when you called him on it.'

'When I asked him about his name change and his first wife Mary, he nearly had a second heart attack on the spot. I explained to him that if the case regarding the three girls ever came to court, then their defence lawyers would look to blacken his character by digging up any dirt, they could find on him.' Heather continued smugly. 'Oh, I also officially made him aware of his rights and persisted that if there was anything, he needed to tell the police that he should do so now. I've never seen the colour drain from someone's face so quick. In seconds Fred formally known as Frank dropped his case and withdrew the charges against you right out of the blue. He also insisted that he was feeling a lot better and was now unsure of what took place that Saturday night and that maybe he was mistaken about the whole ordeal—he couldn't get rid of me quick enough,' she scoffed.

Jamie couldn't believe what she was hearing; she was not used to things going her way and still had a few doubts. 'What about the CCTV footage though, won't that still have to be dealt with and cleared up?'

'What CCTV footage? I destroyed that a long time ago. No one saw it but me.'

Jamie was so relieved that she had climbed out of the mess unscathed, all thanks to Heather that she didn't want to deter the kisses that she had started to receive from her. Eventually, though, she felt that she had to push her away as the curiosity about her marriage was getting the better of her.

'Heather, I went to the station to look for you today and...' she didn't quite know how to put it. The woman had just put her job in jeopardy by stopping the charges against her, and now, she was about to dig a hole between them—again. 'Well—I met your husband—who seemed like a nice guy and very much still married to you.'

Heather turned on her heels to look away for a moment. Not knowing what would fall from her mouth in reply. 'I never lied to you, Jamie; you knew that I was Mrs Williams now, didn't you? It's not like we were going to sail off into the sunset together and spend the rest of our lives rekindling our teens,' she paused for a few seconds and caught Jamie's stare. 'God, I hope you didn't think that—it was just you seemed like the type that wouldn't worry about a husband being hidden away at home. Christ Jamie, I'm so sorry if I led you to believe that in any way....'

'No—not for one moment' Jamie interrupted, 'I just thought it would have been good to understand what was actually happening here. You're right. I'm not about commitment of any kind and would probably have let you down like I have all the others pretty soon, anyway.'

Jamie had tried to convince herself that this was true. It was not that she had fallen back in love with Heather, more in lust with her. Although she probably would have had a go at a relationship, which would have been something that she had never really tried before.

Heather could see that she had probably misjudged the situation and broke the awkward silence. 'I do really like you Jamie and you have always held a special place in my heart, but my marriage and my work go hand in hand. My husband has had affairs as well, but we never mention it. We try to keep our marriage open if we need to, with a stressful job like ours it helps to release the pressure sometimes. I'm sorry Jamie this sounds so awful. Please don't let us lose a friendship over it.'

Jamie reassured Heather that this wouldn't affect how close they had become again and went their separate ways for the night.

* * *

Jamie couldn't keep it to herself any longer about being off the hook with the taxi driver and told Sam. She felt guilty as her old friend cried over the phone with relief. Sam had felt too old at thirty-five to be worrying about doing time and had other things planned, like meeting up with the new girl at work.

During the lengthy conversation that went on well into the night, Sam had told Jamie in detail of her bungled chat up lines that had seemed to have fallen on deaf ears until she agreed to go out with her. Jamie was pleased for Sam; she needed a break in her absent love life if only to stop worrying about Jamie's.

Their conversation kept going back to Jamie meeting up with her old teacher, and Sam had noticed that Jamie must have mentioned Sarah's name over fifty times in the last hour. It was as if she couldn't control her need to talk about her. This was a new experience for Jamie. She had never seemed that interested in anyone before, and Sam knew it. She kept ribbing her about it each time by calling Sarah 'Mrs Suburbia.' Sam was right about her mentioning Sarah, though. Heather's revelation had only taken up seconds of their talk time and them staying as friends felt like an OK situation for them both. She hadn't felt the need to dwell on any feelings she may have had for her school sweetheart.

When she finally put her head on the pillow, sleep evaded her as she couldn't stop thinking of Sarah. After tossing and turning and checking her mobile every ten minutes for the time, she got out of bed to email her estate agent. She didn't quite know why, but she felt a need to ask if the property on Maidstone Hill was still for sale. It would be worth a try. Even if this rekindling infatuation with Sarah was just sparked by an old school-girl crush, she felt it would be nice to live in such a respectable, quiet neighbourhood for a change. Having them as neighbours would also be a bonus, of course.

Unexpectedly, the agent was still awake, and the email was answered straight away. They arranged for her to see the property first thing in the morning, and Jamie would have to try to sleep on her new plans for the future until then.

The estate agent was late as usual, and Jamie sat in her car wondering which property on this leafy row of houses was up for sale as she could see no signs displayed. They were all new builds so structurally and cosmetically she wouldn't have any problem in moving straight in if the price were right. She had decided she would visit Sarah afterwards to explain about the case being dropped as to let her know that Zoe was in the clear. She was looking forward to seeing them both again, and she felt it as an ache in her stomach.

Thirty minutes later than arranged a brand-new Lexus pulled up behind her and flashed its lights. As they both got out of their cars and joined each other in a handshake, Jane Carlton made her apologies. She then gave a false smile, brushed her breakfast crumbs off her Jacket and pulled down her tight skirt. It was two sizes too small and had risen to meet her protruding belly.

'I had to eat on the run this morning Miss Taylor we seem to be having a busy day regarding this property and someone else wants to view it straight after you.'

Jamie thought this as a likely story, as they usually said that to hurry a decision if you were considering buying the property.

Jamie followed the estate agent further down to the end of the street and as she led her up the familiar path, she felt sick to her stomach.

'It's this one—number 165, it has a tenant at the moment but it's only a short lease, so it won't be a problem. She knew that it was to be put up for sale sometime soon and was told to leave it vacant this morning for viewings.'

She followed as Jane Carlton tried to squeeze herself through Sarah and Molly's beautiful home. This time she felt like an intruder. It was only yesterday that she had heard Sarah say how much she loved living there, and now it was on the market for sale without a care for the soon to be homeless people within.

Molly's toys were set up in their neat little scenarios, waiting for her to return. The guilt washed over her as they went to view upstairs; Jamie was faced with photographs of Molly at different stages of her little life lining the walls. This was not just a house for sale, this was a home, and without giving it another thought Jamie made the split decision to buy it as to not let anyone else tear this home away from her newly found friends.

Jane drove them both back to the offices of Carlton and Carlton, and they put in an offer on the house without hesitation. It was for the exact asking price and the seller accepted it with an informal yes over the phone. It left Jamie in shock. She had set out that day to buy a house to live in and had now purchased a property with sitting tenants that she had no intention of kicking out.

As she tried to make sense of her rash decision, she figured that another few years with Michael wouldn't be that bad. She had always lived in hope that he would find someone not so Mafia-like to settle down with, and she always liked to keep him close.

Michael still had a thing for bad boys and had got himself tangled up in something that gave him nightmares for weeks not so long ago. He was seeing Mario—actual name Marlon, who came from a family with a lot of dodgy connections. Expensive suits and fast cars were the main attraction to Michael, and Mario kept him as his 'bitch' for three months.

The relationship was intense, and Jamie saw Michael turn into a nervous wreck, always looking over his shoulder. She was relieved when it was over, and Mario went back to playing the straight guy by moving in with his *proper girlfriend*. This was the longest relationship that Michael had had to date, and when it was all over, he went back to his casual encounters and one-night stands.

When Jamie returned to her car, she decided to hang around to give Sarah the news about the house. She felt a little apprehensive as Sarah pulled into the driveway and didn't know how to approach the subject. She hoped that she would be happy enough but didn't want to seem like she was getting involved with something that was none of her business.

As she approached, she could tell that Sarah had been crying. She unlocked the door and ushered Molly to run inside the house before her. She took her bag from the boot of the car, then as she closed it down, she noticed Jamie standing there.

'Oh, Hi Jamie, sorry, but I'm not good company at the moment—I've had some bad news about the house.' As the tears broke through, Jamie put her arm around her and helped her in through the door.

'Hey Sarah, it's OK–I have good news, I couldn't let them do it to you.'

Sarah looked confused, stopped crying and dried her eyes. 'Jamie—I don't understand—do what?'

She explained about the sale and the fact that she still wanted it to be her and Molly's home for as long as they needed it. Jamie tried to paint it as if it were an investment on her part and no big deal as she could wait for another house and use the rental money to pay the mortgage, but Sarah could see the goodness in her and was ecstatic by her actions. This had been Molly's home for most of her life, and the thought of losing it just for those few hours today had ripped Sarah to the core.

Jamie invited them both out for lunch to celebrate of which they accepted. They sold it to Molly by a promise of taking her to the playground afterwards, so it was a done deal in the little girl's eyes.

As she played on her own in the sandpit, Jamie explained about the other good news of the day and about the double-dealing taxi driver's bigamist ways. This was another reason for Sarah to be thankful that her new friend had come into her life.

'I'll never be able to repay you for what you did today Jamie, myself and Molly will always be indebted to you and your kindness.' Jamie tried to shrug it off. She wasn't used to situations like this and the day had felt like a blur. She knew she had done the right thing though as soon as she saw a smile return to Sarah's face.

'The landlord mentioned to me a few months ago that he might have to sell, but as they put no signs up and we had no estate agent's calling, I hung on to the hope that he had changed his mind. The phone call from them this morning shocked me. I was in no position to just up and move. You've really saved me from an impossible situation.'

'There's no need to thank me, Sarah. I just did what I thought was right. I was looking to invest in a property in this area, anyway. It was lucky for me I have such great long-term tenants to look after it.'

Later that evening they were still enjoying getting to know each other, and Jamie had been invited back for a bottle of wine. When Molly had finished playing with her toys on the floor, she jumped onto the sofa next to her, edging her way closer to Jamie. She lifted Molly onto her lap and gave her a big hug under the thankful eye of a smiling Sarah.

'You do realise that you're stuck with me visiting from time to time now—and sometimes I can get very annoying.' She tickled Molly into a giggling state.

'You are welcome here anytime, Jamie. We love seeing you, don't we Molly?'

Molly gave a big yawn, and Sarah took the sleepy bundle in her arms.

'I'll expect that bottle of wine open when I come back down Miss Taylor—say goodnight to Jamie Molly.'

Molly waved with one eye open and didn't protest to being taken to bed. Running around the park all day had taken its toll.

Jamie did as she was told and opened the single bottle of low alcohol wine to share with Sarah. This was not the hard liquor she was used to drinking but knew that with a child in the house this was the responsible thing to do and she admired Sarah for that. Her parents would have been too drunk to notice that the kids were not in the house, let alone in bed. Most of the time, even at a young age, Jamie would carry Michael to bed and read him a bedtime story. She would make it up as she went along, as she could barely decipher the words herself.

Chapter 15

Heather had been restless all night from feeling guilty about her chat with Jamie yesterday. Her married life was something she saw as an open affair, and she was not used to being questioned about her actions. The time she had spent getting to know Jamie again had been closure on the past for her, and she had enjoyed being in her company. Knowing, as an adult, how bad she must have suffered growing up in a family with domestic violence made her realise how different their upbringings really were. Working with families of abuse throughout her career had given her good counselling skills; maybe she could help repair the relationship that Jamie had with her mother? If that was at all possible. At the least, she could open some doors of communication between them, she thought.

She managed to grab herself a spare hour at work to see if she could gather further information on how the

Taylor's were doing and if there had been any new enquiries. The domestic abuse calls had stopped coming to the station around Christmas of last year but digging deeper she found that a missing person's report had been opened on James Taylor shortly after that.

As she sat at her desk with her screen on display, Inspector Stokes with his comb-over hair and 70s suit took an interest over her shoulder. Whilst continuously chewing on day-old gum, he tapped the screen with a greasy finger.

'They flagged this guy up last week as a possible found. He drowned in a quarry. The rats had had a munch at his face so they couldn't say it was him for definite, but they were doing all the regular checks.'

Heather's first instinct was to run straight to Jamie and tell her what had happened, but without definite proof, she didn't want to alarm her to what was going on just yet. Instead, she decided to go back to her hometown. She knew what that monster looked like and had a good chance as anyone to identifying him.

* * *

The one thing that she couldn't get used to with being a police officer, was the trip to the morgue. Normally she would avoid it at all costs and send someone else, but this time she knew she had to see it through for Jamie's sake. It was as cold as death, and the greyness of the brick walls against the shiny steel boxes questioned mortality.

When she spoke to the officers in charge, she learned that the case had moved on and they had already made a formal identification and it was indeed James Taylor senior that they had laid out on the slab. The forensics had not had an easy job as the water from the quarry had bloated his body, but the wedding ring he was wearing was a positive enough identification to start as it had his and Sheila's name engraved on it. They later matched his fingerprints with the ones on file and made a positive identification.

Heather still had some friends at the station from when she was working there in her early days, so the information was running freely with those dealing with the case. They explained to her that when the news got out that they had found a man in the quarry; they had tried to contact Sheila Taylor about her husband but could not find her at her address. This was noted as unusual for her as she very rarely went out anywhere. They were not looking for her as a suspect, just yet, but would like to ask her some questions about the last time that she saw her husband.

Heather explained to her colleagues that the deceased's daughter Jamie was an old friend of hers and had reassured them she would tell her and Michael of what had happened to their father. She knew that Jamie had always hated him. But death has a different effect on people's emotions. She had found this out so many times in her line of work.

The following evening hit hard. Heather had brought Jamie and Michael together in the club to relay the terrible news about their abusive father. But what seemed even harder was that after all the years that their poor mother had suffered at the hands of that man, he was now the victim, and she knew that they would soon be looking at Sheila as a possible suspect. Heather kept this hidden from the siblings and implied that it was only to rule her out of their enquiries, but Jamie could see it on her face that she knew what was coming next. The question of her whereabouts had to be dealt with as a matter of urgency, so Heather tried to get the ball rolling with a gentle approach.

'It will be better for her if you two find her first. Are there any relatives or friends that your mother may have gone to?'

Michael was appalled and felt that Heather had his mother under suspicion.

'There is no fucking way that my mother would have had anything to do with this. You're looking at it all wrong. She's probably out looking for him now. She was that devoted to him—did any of you even think of that?'

He slammed the door and left. This was too much for him to take, and he needed time to think.

'You can't honestly think that she had anything to do with this Heather—do you? You've seen the size of him to her. Besides, she would have done it ages ago if that was the case.'

'I'm not saying that Jamie, I'm only trying to help. When they summon you and your brother down to the station that will be the first question they ask you...'

Jamie interrupted quite harshly 'So did he drown? Or what?' Tears welled in her eyes, but she was torn between anger and relief as to the reason. She couldn't bring herself to grieve for him. That would be ridiculous. She just had to get it straight in her head that he had gone. 'The quarry is only twenty metres away from the back of the house. Maybe he had got himself so pissed that he just fell in. Maybe there was nobody else involved. Have they thought of that?'

She wiped the tears away with the sleeve of her shirt hard across her face, biting down on her lip as if to stop herself from screaming.

'This could all be a huge mistake, he was always falling over, pissed, that's how this has happened most definitely. My mother wouldn't have had anything to do with this!' Jamie screamed.

The mixture of grief and abandonment that she had felt from her mother's choice to stay with him was raising its head. Now she wanted to blame her for everything. If she had left him in the first place, things would have been different. They would have had better lives maybe even him, she thought. She came to her senses and recalled his behaviour. There would have been no chance of running away knowing how controlling he was. She would never have escaped the house to even try. Her mind kept racing with hopeless scenarios. The fact was, he was dead, that bastard was dead. The father that she had once loved, that had once held her in his arms and comforted her when she fell off a swing, was dead. But the fear of him was still very much alive.

As she sat alone in the flat, she tried to put her broken head back together. It grieved her to a certain extent, but not how someone should grieve for their parent. She regretted that she hadn't got the chance to tell him as an adult of how much of a pathetic, bullying human being he was through all of Jamie's childhood. The fact that her mother was supposedly missing was also laying heavy on her mind. It was no use she knew she would have to go back to the estate and find her.

* * *

As she pulled into her old street with her brand-new car and brand-new personality, she could picture her old man waiting for her on the gate, ready to give her a clip round the ear for anything he chose to mention. The full moon was low in the night sky and as she closed her eyes, she took a deep breath of the air that she had grown up breathing. The same dank smell of weeds from the quarry mixed with the stale smell of the social club on the corner at kicking out time tarnished the moment.

Her old house was staring back at her, willing her to enter. She still had a key and prayed that the locks hadn't been changed. She was in luck.

The place looked the same as when she had first left but felt a lot smaller. The stuff in her old room untouched. A rizla packet with Heather's phone number on the back lay wrapped in time on her bedside table awaiting her return. Her mam and dad's old room still smelled of vomit and fags, same as it always did. She could picture herself jumping on the bed when she was small and hiding under it when playing a game of hide and seek.

As she approached Michael's old room, she noticed that someone had ripped the door off the hinges. She eased it to one side to enter, finding that someone had turned the place over. It looked as though it had been in a raid. There was nothing left. The bedspread was hardly recognisable. It appeared as if someone had started a fire on it, then doused it with water as a better idea.

She went back down the familiar stairs, confident that the last two would creak, of which they did. The house returned to silence as she noticed her mother's handbag at the side of her living room chair with her purse, fags and lighter still inside. She feared the worst. Her mother would never have left without it. She always had it glued to her side. She would even take it to the bathroom with her in fear of her father pinching the housekeeping money to spend on booze.

Looking out of the window at Ricky's old house brought a lot of painful memories to mind. She had seen one of his brothers a few years back and was told how Ricky's dad had nursed his poor wife with cancer alone in the house until she finally died in his arms on Christmas day. She had planned it that way with just the two of them, with none of the kids around. As soon as cancer ruined her abilities, she banned her children from the house. She wanted them to remember her as the mother she once was, strong and burly, not the empty, lifeless shell she had become. He said that his father had found comfort in the thought that it had reunited her with her precious boy, and that that was the only thing that kept him going after she passed.

Jamie figured it wouldn't do any harm to visit him, so she made the same journey that she did every day of her childhood to Ricky's front door.

As she knocked, she noticed the letter R that Ricky had keyed into the paintwork around the window frame and remembered his mam slapping him around the ear for doing it.

She cupped her hands over her eyes and pressed her face against the opaque glass to see if there was any movement. At first, she thought that no one was in, but on the second knock, Tom Webster appeared, holding the door on the chain with a shaky hand.

'Go away, we're not buying anything, and we have nothing to give now piss off.'

Jamie tried to make herself seen through the crack of the door and hoped that Tom Webster would recognise her.

'Mr Webster—it's me, Jamie—Jamie Taylor.'

He recognised her voice at once and opened the door to welcome her in.

'My, my Jamie, you have grown into a beautiful creature. I suppose you're here looking for your mother, are you? Come on in.'

The man had aged drastically, and she could see the years of heartache etched on his face. She hadn't seen him much since Ricky died, as it wasn't long after that, that she left school and moved away. He was often in her thoughts though; every time Michael did something out of the ordinary, she wondered whether this had been a trait from his biological dad.

He led Jamie into the living room and there sat on the sofa with her back to the door was her mother, Sheila Taylor.

'Hey, Sheila—you have a visitor, love.'

As she turned to see who it was, the burn scars that were trailing her mother's face startled Jamie. They had healed and looked like they had been there for a while but were still shocking to see for the first time.

'Jamie—sweetheart—is that really you?'

She blurted with tears like a blubbering toddler. Jamie couldn't understand a word her mother was saying all she could do was hold her in her arms and cradle her through her misery, joining in with the flow of tears. She hadn't cried like that in a long time, and her eyes were making up for all the lost years. Tom Webster left them to it and went into the kitchen to put the kettle on as Sheila lit up a fag and took a deep drag.

'He's gone, Jamie—your father, my Jimmy, he's gone—and I know I should be relieved, but I'm not. I know that I was weak and let you kids down, but inside that torn and twisted body was the man I once adored. You are part of him, and when you were born he would have given you the moon from the sky if he could. I knew it would end in a bad way as it was always on the card's, but I still can't let him go.'

'I know Mam—I heard. Do you know what happened? Do you know that the police are looking to question you?'

Sheila slammed her hands down on the arms of her chair, 'I can't tell them about any of this Jamie it's our business no one else's!'

Even though he was gone, she was still living by his rules; a family should be kept private, and what goes on in a man's house was his own business and not for public knowledge.

Sheila rocked back and forth and took a long, hard drag on her fag before telling Jamie about their last moments together.

'There was nothing I could do. He was so strong. He started a fire on Michael's bed, then pushed me into it.

I scrambled to the floor, but then he grabbed me again and kept pushing my face towards it. My hair was on fire, my clothes smouldering, and he was still screaming at me.' She outed her fag into the overflowing ashtray and stared into space before continuing. 'That night was the last time I saw him. A few weeks later, Tom drove me to the police station to tell them he was missing. They said that they would put it on their files and not to worry; in situations like this people turn up eventually, especially when they run out of money.'

'He probably realised he had gone too far by burning you and did a runner before it involved the police.' Jamie added.

'No Jamie, someone pulled him off me, but I couldn't see who with all the smoke. My hair was still on fire, so I was desperately trying to put it out—but I knew that someone pulled him off me. I could hear mumbled arguing going on but couldn't make out the voice'

She tried to focus on Jamie's face but saw the reflection of her Jimmy staring back at her. 'I didn't tell the police about the fire, I'd rather me die right now than tell anyone your father's business—whoever pulled him off me put the fire out before they left, and if they hadn't, it would have burnt the whole house down with me in it. The police didn't need to know that.'

Jamie pulled herself up from her mother and told her to rest for a bit. The picture of her being in that situation as helpless as she was brought bile to her mouth, so she left for the kitchen to take stock of what she had learnt.

She took a few deep breaths in as not to succumb to the anger she had boiling inside her. Tom handed her a cup of strong tea and put his hand on her shoulder.

'Before you say it, Jamie, I didn't see who the chancer was either. I would've burnt the bastard alive if I'd have caught him holding your mother down like that it's brutal. Aye, the first thing that I knew about it was when Sheila was banging on my door screaming. My first instinct was to get her inside. You know what this lot are like around here they all think they are Holy Joe's. She wouldn't let me call the fire brigade as she insisted the fire was out. So, the place then was how you see it now. Only a damn site hotter.'

Jamie believed him, as she had always found him a straight-talking man. 'So, do you have any idea of what went on, Tom? And how he ended up in the quarry?'

'He was a very hated man around these parts, Jamie, and there were many people that would have quite happily seen him dead. It was bad enough when you and your brother were here, but when you both left, the eejit only had her to take his anger out on so that wee lass was getting beatings daily,' he looked into the room at Sheila and lowered his voice, 'Of course, your mother would deny everything to the peelers as she always did. He would stop for a day or two or lie low for a while—but he always came back twice as nasty.'

Jamie felt an overwhelming burden of guilt, 'Christ—I should have been here—I worried that if he knew we were in contact, it would have made things worse for her.

Thanks, Tom, you've been a good friend to her over the years. I don't know what she would have done without having you to run to.' She drank her tea, then asked the question that she never thought she would ever say. 'Has she said anything to you about moving on without him?' he shook his head, 'We can't impose on you like this it's not fair, I'll get her things together and take her back with me until this is all sorted....'

Tom interrupted, 'I don't mind Jamie; she can stay here as long as she needs too. It's nice to have the company, to be honest. I know you probably want her with you now, but I don't think she wants to leave. When I explained to her, they had found a body, and that there was a good chance that it may be him, she just stared into space.'

'She probably wouldn't accept it. I'm glad that you were the one to tell her.' she said gratefully.

Tom did a quick check on Sheila and closed the kitchen door. 'I didn't want her to hear it from anyone else you know what this place is like for the craic. They can't keep their lazy gobs shut, always putting people down and adding to what they think is the truth—and this has been the craic of the year.'

Same old estate, Jamie thought, unhappily knowing that things hadn't changed.

Tom took the empty teacups to the sink, rinsed them under the tap and listened by the door. He whispered out of respect for Sheila. 'The thing is, even though she knows he's dead, she still acts like he's coming back.

The lass is always looking over her shoulder and watching what she says. It's probably the shock. Why don't you leave her with me for a few more days love and then maybe she'll see things clearer?'

Tom was right. Sheila wasn't budging. Jamie told her mam that she would be back again tomorrow and then every day after that to be there for her. But the words seemed to drift into the air rather than be taken in by her confused mother. She just sat there staring at a blank television screen.

As Tom saw her to the door, he gave her a hug and some much-needed reassurance. 'Don't worry, Jamie, you know I'll take good care of her. I wouldn't harm a hair on a woman's head, especially not your mother.'

She would do as she said and return tomorrow but keeping her mother's whereabouts from the police would be something that she would have to think long and hard about.

Chapter 16

The meeting with Carlton and Carlton went well under the circumstances, and Jamie had bought herself a house. All that was needed was a few final signatures, and she would legally be the landlord of a much-loved home. It had been a week since she was told the news about her father, and although she had made the journey to see her mother enough times, she had spent most of the time with Sarah and Molly.

Sarah had been very consoling about the news of her father's passing, and Jamie had felt a comforting need for her and Molly's company. Every moment spent with them felt a touch closer to normal, and she needed that to stop herself from totally cracking up. The tenancy agreement was in front of them, ready to be signed, then they would officially be tied to each other by paper at least. But at the back of Jamie's mind, she knew she had deeper feelings enfolding of wanting more than just friendship.

'So, are you sure about this agreement Jamie of not needing this place for yourself? I understand if you want to change your mind.'

'Of course not. This is yours and Molly's home for as long as you need it. I've put my plans on hold of finding a new place as I need to spend more time with my brother. Although, you would think that nothing has happened by the way he's been acting.'

Michael had turned up at the club last night for his show, and that was the first time she had seen him since they were told about their father. Countless messages had been left for him to contact her, but he didn't want to know. She managed to get a few minutes with him in between costume changes, but that wasn't long enough to go into detail about their mother. It had felt good forgetting herself for a while. She had been someone else, someone without a care in the world, but now she had to face the gruelling reality of life. Telling her brother she had been to see their mam and letting him know about the fire was something she wasn't looking forward to. But she had to let him know, as the police would soon call them in for questioning. They needed to sit down as a family and work things out. She told him that he couldn't hide away from it forever, and he promised to catch up with her later that evening.

Jamie spent the rest of the morning with Sarah alone as Molly was at the childminders until early evening.

They had spent the day shopping, drinking coffee and talking about everything other than Jamie, as that's the way she wanted it. When it was time for Jamie to drop Sarah home, neither of them wanted to leave each other's company. As they pulled onto the driveway, they still had so much to say it seemed. Although they both had quite different backgrounds, they were similar in their outlook on life and had many things in common.

As the time drew closer for them to part, Jamie leaned over to open the door for Sarah, but as she did Sarah put her hand on top to stop her. Turning to face each other, it was obvious that the feelings she had for her were mutual and Jamie leaned in for a kiss. Sarah responded, not quite as confident as Jamie at first, but as the kiss lasted longer, they both fell deeper into the moment. The windows on the inside of the car had steamed up from the heat that their bodies created, and they both knew that this was leading to something more intimate. Jamie didn't want her first time with Sarah to be like this. She whispered to her about taking this inside and although Sarah was incredibly nervous about agreeing; she went to the bedroom willingly.

Jamie took everything slowly as not to overwhelm Sarah, asking her if she was OK with every touch that Jamie placed on her body. They sat facing each other on the bed enjoying each other's gaze and after taking off her t-shirt she gently removed Sarah's, only losing eye contact for a split second. They both lay on the bed and Jamie slowly unbuttoned her trousers. Sarah trembled nervously under Jamie's hand, but as she entered her, she sighed, pushing her nails tightly into Jamie's back. This caused Jamie to cry out in passion, inviting her to please Sarah more. Then for the first time, Sarah placed her hands upon a woman, *her* woman not knowing quite where it would lead but confident enough to more than try. Each caress, each kiss was important and carefully thought out by both. They were glistening wet with the heat as they writhed beneath the soft white cotton sheets. Both girls begged for release as they climaxed together, and as they both lay back in exhaustion, Jamie could feel a tear run down her cheek. Her face blushing for the first time. She had never experienced such tenderness and knew that this was bigger than a lunchtime rendezvous.

Lust always led sex for Jamie, love never had a mention. This felt different, this *was* making love, the experience had no boundaries. They held each other tight, as if letting go would let the rest of the world in, and kissed for what seemed like an hour. Both knew that this was no mistake, as they felt so easy in each other's company. They shared no embarrassing after chat or felt the need for either of them to leave as everything felt right. There was no reason to join the rest of the world, just yet.

* * *

When Jamie eventually arrived home, Michael was waiting for her as promised. She didn't feel the need to share any details of her afternoon with him as she wanted to keep the memory private, and to herself. Michael would probably turn it into something seedy, and she didn't want that for her beautiful Sarah.

'Sorry for disappearing, Jamie. I wasn't ready to talk about him. It makes me sick just thinking about it all. But he deserved all he got. I can't grieve for someone I hated as much as he hated me.'

'I know it's hard, Michael, but we have to think of Mam. She's on the edge. It's like she can't accept that he's not coming back, and if she doesn't speak to the police, it will look like she has something to hide. I didn't get the chance to tell you everything about the fire when we talked last night as I didn't want to unnerve you, but she told me that there was someone else in the house with them that night and they pulled him off her. I hate to think of what would have happened if they hadn't stopped him. He would have probably killed her this time. She has burn marks all over her face, Michael, and she will find it hard to hide that from the police. They will know that there is more to it as soon as they see her. And that someone who pulled him off probably knows exactly what happened next.'

'But if she didn't see who it was Jamie, then there is no point in mentioning it to the police is there, they can't force information out of her if she doesn't have any. She has been lying to the police all her life, so what difference will it make if she keeps quiet this one last time? Just leave her be Jamie. They will see that it's nothing to do with her and move on.' Michael sounded convincing, but Jamie knew that it would not be that easy, especially after the fire.

'What if they don't though and try to pin it on her? It won't take them long to work out that he was trying to burn her that night as your bedroom looks like a bomb has gone off in there. I'm going to have a word with Heather tomorrow and see what she thinks about it all. Maybe if Mam tells the police, they may have a chance of catching whoever killed him.'

'No, Jamie—don't get anyone else involved it's too risky.'

Jamie looked confused, 'too risky for who?'

'Too risky for me—I saw him that night. I know I should have said something at the time, but I couldn't. He wasn't going to ruin my life like he did my childhood.' Michael sat down and put his face in his hands.

'I was asked to do a gig in the White Hart just down the road from our old school. He never drinks in there, so I thought that I would be safe. How wrong could I be? It all started off OK, and then he stumbled in halfway through. As soon as he saw it was me on the stage, he went ballistic, hurling abuse at me and throwing chairs and tables around. The bouncers kicked him out before he could do any actual damage. But I wasn't going to let him get away with it. I was so fired up Jamie I was shocked at myself, so when I finished the gig, I followed him back home.'

Jamie poured him a whisky. She could see that his hands were shaking and didn't want him to stop. He downed the glass in a second and continued in despair.

'When I got to the house, I saw that he had Mam upstairs and was burning all the photos of me on the bed. He was screaming at her like a madman and accusing her of being too soft on me when we were growing up. He said it was her fault that I turned into a Nancy boy and that she had probably encouraged it just to wind him up. They couldn't see me as they had their backs to the door, but when he pushed her face down into the fire, I couldn't just stand there and let it happen, I had to do something—so it was me Jamie—I pulled him off her and pushed him away. He smashed his face on the bedside table, but it wasn't enough to kill him, just gave him a bloody nose. I was still in drag, so Mam wouldn't have recognised me anyway in all the commotion. I chucked a bucket of water over her and the bed, and luckily the fire went out. I was terrified, I thought he would kill us both.'

Michael's words hit hard. But he was her baby brother, and she had spent a lot of her life protecting him, and she wasn't going to stop now.

'You did the right thing, Michael. He probably would have killed the both of you if you hadn't stopped him. How the hell did you get out of there?'

'He got back on his feet and pushed passed me. After I outed the fire, I looked for him all over the house, but he was nowhere to be seen. He just disappeared.

As I got outside, Mario was standing there waiting for me. He practically pushed me into the car and sped off. He was supposed to pick me up from the club, so he must have followed me back there. I don't know what happened next Jamie, honest. Mario always had the boys with him following behind in another car, so I thought that maybe he had something to do with it. But I didn't think they would fucking kill him. At most they might have driven him somewhere and give him a kicking, I wasn't expecting him to have done this. Mario finished with me not long after that, so I felt it safer not to ask any questions.'

Jamie stood up and started pacing. She was less worried about the police now and more worried about Mario's family finding out about him and Michael if it all came out.

'For fuck's sake, why didn't you tell me at the time? We could have sorted this out together...'

Michael interrupted. 'I couldn't tell you. Mario said that I was not to tell anyone that I had been back to the house or there would be consequences. You know what you're like you would have gone straight over there. It was better for us if it was just forgotten. So, for god's sake, don't let Mam say anything—OK.'

'How do you know that you haven't been seen already? I've only just had a near escape myself with being caught on camera. They are fucking everywhere these days.'

Michael shrugged his shoulders. 'I don't know Jamie, but I'm sure as hell not going to offer myself up as a suspect. If they have evidence, then I will deal with it when they come for me. Until then, they will have to keep guessing. Anyway, there are bound to be at least ten people out there that would give him a kicking just for the hell of it. It doesn't mean to say that it was someone he knew well.'

Unfortunately, Jamie knew this to be true. She had visited her mother every day, as promised. And for the first time in her life, she could visualise some sort of future for her away from the man that had beaten her senseless for most of her life. She didn't need the hassle of the police digging into her business, but she knew that she would have to talk to them at some point. Michael had shocked her with his revelation, and she had no idea how to handle it.

'You're gonna have to talk to Mario and warn him about all this in case the police find out it happened on that night.'

Michael cocked his head. 'I know this! But I'd rather wait until I have to. I don't want him freaking out on me. He has his new straight life now and he wouldn't want me bringing up his sordid past, as he would put it. You know what his family are like—they think they are the Welsh Krays they wouldn't think twice about shutting me up in any way they see fit.'

Jamie didn't want to put Michael under any more stress. She promised to keep his secret for as long as he needed her to. The police would probably find out anyway as people on the estate talk, and someone was bound to have seen him storming through the streets in a dress. Keeping this information away from Heather was going to be difficult. Now that she had started helping them, Jamie knew that she would make it her duty to find out what had happened to their father. She couldn't ask her to stop her enquiries as it would look too suspicious. She would have to be more careful in the information that she shared with her.

* * *

The three missed calls from Heather were still flashing away on Jamie's mobile phone and she knew that if she didn't call her back soon, she would be caught off guard with a visit. If she were going to lie about not knowing anything about her dad's disappearance, she would rather do it over the phone than to her face as she knew she had never been a very convincing liar.

'Hey, Heather—sorry I missed your calls I misplaced my phone for a while. Is everything OK with you?'

'Yeah fine—I was going to come to the club and see you, but after the way, we left things last time I didn't know whether I would be welcome...' Heather paused, waiting for an answer from Jamie that never came. 'I know I haven't been in touch for us to spend any time together, but it's a bit hard when I've been working on the case of your father. The boss doesn't like any heavy personal involvement. I told him we were in school together but obviously, that was as far as I took it—Jamie are you still there?'

Jamie eventually spoke 'Yes—yes, I understand, you don't have to explain. It's not as if we were an item or anything.'

'Thanks for understanding Jamie. I just wanted to keep you up to date with what happened to your father. The police have tracked down your mother and although she knows next to nothing regarding the disappearance, she has helped us piece a few things together. They have traced him on CCTV the night that your mother said she last saw him, and it looks like his last known appearance was at the White Hart. We spoke to the bouncers there, and they explained that they had to kick him out as he was upsetting the customers and hailing abuse at the stage act. We were lucky the camera on High Street was working and we could clearly see that he was making his way back home. He kicked a few wheelie bins on the way, and you could tell by his body language that he was angered about being thrown out of the pub. But he was not as drunk in his walk as we would have expected him to be. He probably went straight home after that. But as there are no cameras on the estate, that's the last footage, we have of him. Are you OK with me telling you about this or would you rather me stop?'

'No, don't stop. I want to know everything. The more details I know, the better. If I can explain to my mam exactly what happened, it may give her more of a chance to accept things. I know it seems crazy, but I don't think she is taking any of this in, she still acts as if he's coming back.'

Heather sounded confused 'I don't understand—have you seen her then?'

Jamie knew that silence wouldn't get her out of this one, so she answered unwillingly. 'Yes—sorry—I thought I'd said....'

'No, Jamie—you hadn't mentioned it. I wish you had, as we have wasted a lot of time looking for her.'

Heather's voice had now gone over to police mode, and Jamie knew that she could drop everyone in it if she made any more slip-ups like that.

Heather continued 'We now have the coroner's report, and it shows that he was dead before he hit the water, probably from a blow to the back of his head, so we know he didn't jump in the quarry himself. The coroner also said that he had significant burns on his hands, but when they mentioned it to your mother, she explained that she had fallen asleep on the bed looking at photographs with a cigarette in her mouth and that he burnt his hands waking her up and outing the fire. She said he went out after that as normal and that was the last time, she saw him.'

Jamie jumped in to back up her mother's statement 'That's what she said to me. He just went out for a drink the same as usual and didn't come back. He's done that before, turning up days later so she wouldn't have worried about it straight away.'

Jamie tried to diffuse the truth as much as she could, so it didn't look like her mother was lying.

'That's the impression I got. Look, Jamie, I'm afraid that they are now treating this as a murder enquiry, so they will need to speak to her in more detail. If you could ask her if she can try to remember anything else about that night—anything that might have been out of the ordinary—even if it's the smallest thing it might seem insignificant to her, but it could be an important lead to us...'

Jamie interrupted. 'I understand, and I'll let her know. But I very much doubt that she knows anything else. Thanks for taking such an interest in this Heather, but you don't have to spend all your spare time helping us out.'

'That's OK, Jamie. It's not my spare time anymore, as they have asked me to work on the case officially. As I know you, and the area, they thought it might help. So, you'll probably be seeing a lot more of me, professionally only though, as I explained. So, if you could tell your brother that they need to speak to him and yourself down at the station, that would help.'

Jamie cringed as she heard the words and tried to zip up the situation.

'As I told you before Heather, we haven't seen our parents in a few years so we're not gonna be much help, really.'

'I know you never kept in contact, but they will still want you to give a statement confirming that. They will want to know what type of man he was and if you think he had any enemies. I know it's going to be hard for you both but if you can be as honest as you can without upsetting yourselves it will help.'

Jamie left the conversation there and told Heather she would do as she asked. If they stick to the same story that neither of them had been back to the house, it would be over with quickly. Jamie hoped that maybe they could do their statements together, that way they would both hear what the other was saying.

She tried to switch off from the madness that was swirling around inside her head and as soon as she put the phone down to Heather, she rang Sarah and asked if it was OK for them to spend some time together. Jamie had wanted to tell Sarah everything about what Michael had said, but she knew it would be best for all concerned if she wasn't involved. There were enough people walking around with secrets to carry, and she didn't want to burden Sarah with the load.

It was good to forget about things for a while, spending the rest of the day in the company of her two-favourite people.

Later on that evening, Molly was her usual endearing self and a game of hide-and-seek before bedtime was next on the agenda.

It had ended with a heartfelt request. 'Will you help Mummy put me to bed tonight? And read me my bed-time story?'

Jamie couldn't refuse and gallantly read her way through a story containing princess's brave knights and dragons using the best fairy-tale voices she could muster. She wanted to do her best as not to disappoint Molly. The toddler's eyes battled to stay awake, finally losing halfway through the story. She pulled the bed-cover up and gave her a kiss goodnight. Although she was now asleep, she still gave a little smile before settling down.

Sarah made them both supper, and they sat in front of the TV like an old married couple. Neither of them felt the need for conversation as they were both feeling content with just enjoying each other's company. I could get used to this, Jamie thought as she looked over to her future, I really could.

Chapter 17

Michael was late turning up for his gig at the club and the hen party that had booked in specially to see him was getting restless. They had taken their annoyance out on the barman by grabbing him inappropriately and were already in the bouncer's bad books for dancing on the tables, pouring drinks over each other. She had tried his phone a dozen times, but it just went to voice mail. She persuaded the barman into being a stripper for the night, and this gave her the time she needed for Beefy to arrange for a replacement.

An hour went by and still no Michael. She had contacted every one of his entourage, but no one had seen him. Her next step would have been to call the police if Heather had not called her to go down to the station first. Michael had been taken in for questioning and she had felt it her duty as her friend to explain off the record the details why.

The police had completed an intensive search of Michael's old room at their parent's house where the fire had occurred. They found a size 10 pair of women's shoes wrapped up in a burnt sequined dress at the back of the wardrobe. After closer inspection, they noticed a dry-cleaning tag pinned to the inside of the dress with the date of the fire clearly visible as its collection date. It also had Michael's name and address on its reverse.

As Jamie arrived at the station, she was met by Heather, then taken into a side room for an informal chat. Jamie could tell by her manner and the accompaniment of an assistant P.C that it wasn't good news.

'Thanks for coming Jamie—Please take a seat.' Heather perched herself on the edge of the desk and repeated to her officially the news about Michael. 'I regret to inform you that your brother Michael is helping us with our enquiries regarding your father's murder. He hasn't been charged with anything yet, but it does look like he may have been there on the night your father went missing. We have found the clothes he wore that night in your old house.' She moved closer to Jamie and put her hand on her shoulder. 'He needs to tell us what he knows Jamie, so we can help. Now, all he is saying is 'no comment' to every question, and this is not helping him. We know that he was the Drag Queen appearing at the White Hart that night, and we assume that there may have been an altercation with them later that evening.'

Jamie was convinced that keeping quiet was the right thing to do, but the look on Heather's face made it hard for her to continue with the pretence.

'I don't know what you want me to say—I can't physically make him talk to you...'

'I know this, but the fact that he had changed into his old clothes and had tried to hide his other ones is making him look very suspicious.'

She told the assisting P.C to get her a coffee and lowered her voice upon her leaving.

'Look, Jamie, this could all be totally harmless, and he may have wanted to tone down his appearance when walking through the estate, for example, I get that. But if he doesn't talk to us, it looks bad—it really does. With no hard evidence, we can't legally keep him here, and that is what his solicitor would have probably told him. He is in with him now, so we are waiting to see if he comes to his senses and gives us a reasonable explanation of why he was at the house.'

The P.C returned with coffee and Michael's solicitor. Heather explained to him who Jamie was, and he looked over to her and gave an acknowledging nod.

'Hello, Miss Taylor, my name is Peter Markham, and I have been appointed as your brother's Duty Solicitor. Is it OK if we have a chat? My car is parked outside or if you'd prefer somewhere warmer there is a cafe just down the road?'

'Is he OK? Can I see him?'

'Let's just say we need to have that chat and prefer-
ably out of the station.'

The cafe was the better option and apart from a couple of workmen eating fry ups they were the only ones
in there.

'Your brother has asked me to speak to you on his behalf. Firstly, I must say that he wants you to know that
he had nothing to do with your father's murder and that
the information he gave you regarding that night was
exactly how it happened. He has also explained to me
what happened at the White Heart and how his belongings ended up in the wardrobe of his old room. Anyway,
as it stands your brother hasn't been charged with anything and I have advised him to reply a 'no comment'
when being questioned. Unfortunately, in cases like this,
until the police have someone else in the frame, they
will be hell-bent on making an arrest. Your brother has
explained about the fire and is insistent on saying that
he only intervened to protect his mother on that night.
Now, we need to establish that your father was alive
when Michael last saw him, so we need your mother to
clarify that.'

Jamie was still trying to take it all in, so didn't answer
straight away. Her hands were shaking so much that she
had to put her coffee cup down before she could pull
herself together to answer.

'I understand what you're saying, Mr Markham, but
my mother has already spoken to the police and said
that the fire was all her fault. She said that she had fallen

asleep while smoking and that my father was saving her from getting burned—ridiculous, I know. Won't she get into serious trouble for lying to them?'

Markham shook his head 'No—not necessarily. The police have already got a clear picture of your mother and father's relationship. There is a long history of calls to this address regarding your father hitting your mother. We just need to prove that she lied to protect your father's reputation; same as she's always done.'

The solicitor lowered his voice and Jamie could feel his sympathy for their case. 'The police come up against this a lot, with victims living in denial for years. They blame themselves and protect their abusers. It will simply be passed on to the mental health team to sort out. She won't face any heavy charges. What I need from you is for you to talk to her, explain that by protecting his memory she would be sending her son to prison. The police need to be told that he was still alive when he left that house.'

The solicitor's voice was back to being hard and cold when he read out the duties he would have to perform as a solicitor. She knew that he was only doing his job but having her family life aired with such matter of fact pained her.

As he gathered his papers into his briefcase, his phone rang. After a few brief seconds, the call ended. The look on his face said it all. The forensics had found traces of her father's blood on the clothes that Michael was wearing, and they were now charging him with murder.

* * *

Jamie was still convinced that her father had been the one to blame for all of this. She wondered if he had fallen by the quarry and had simply slid in via the mud. She had tried to talk to Heather about it, but now Michael had been charged with murder it was more than her job at stake if she divulged any information. Whilst back on the estate she reacquainted herself with all the low life and gossips to find out if anyone else had found him lying there and decided to give him a gentle push. Any explanation would suffice in her head if it weren't linked to Michael. She hoped to god that it wasn't Mario and didn't want to be the one accusing him of anything. Even talking to him would be her last decision. She didn't want to involve him unless she had to. He was bound to have someone at the police station in his pocket and would wriggle out of any allegation put to him; so it would only make things worse for Michael.

Her old house was now a crime scene, but that hadn't stopped the neighbours from spray painting the outside. 'Wife beater' and 'Burn in hell' was along the outside wall written as a memorial to the most hated man on the estate. She could barely look at the old place but knew she had to at least try to make her mother break the cycle of protecting her father. Michael needed the backup from her, so the jury would at least think that he was acting heroically rather than maliciously. If he were to be wrongfully imprisoned for his father's death, manslaughter would mean a lot less time inside.

She knocked at the Webster's door and shouted through the letterbox for her mother. Tom's car was parked outside so she knew that they were in, but it seemed that they didn't want to answer. She had hoped that Tom would have spoken to Sheila about speaking to the police on Michael's behalf, but also understood that the Webster's code was not to involve themselves too much in other people's business, and she understood that.

It was no use; she would have to talk to Mario as he was Michael's last chance. If it had been him that killed her father, she knew that he would have covered all tracks as to not link it back to him but there was also a slim chance that he may have still had enough feelings for Michael to not want to see him go down.

Jamie had never been inside Mario's gym. She felt out of place amongst the buff shaven-head bully boys lifting their body weight in steel above their heads. She watched as the barbells were bending from the strain and could smell the sweat mixed with testosterone consuming the air. It was the first time in a long time that she feared for her safety. She wouldn't let it show. All she needed was proof that it couldn't have been Michael that killed her father, for her own sanity to survive, she wasn't there to point the finger at anyone.

She chose one of the smaller lifters to ask where Mario was. After looking her over like a piece of fresh meat, he showed her to the office and told her to wait. They'd covered the walls in muscle-bound posters and pictures of Mario posing with famous boxers and celebrities all proudly displayed in gilded frames. They really were the Welsh Kray's she thought and decided she'd get up and leave. Mario stopped her as he entered the door.

'Sit down, sit down, I won't bite. You're Jamie Taylor, right?'

He didn't allow her the time to answer and told his bodyguard-looking companion to leave them alone and shut the door.

'It's bad what has happened to your brother, but your father was asking for it. You shouldn't treat women that way, it's not clever. Anyway, what can I do for you?'

Jamie didn't know where to begin. She didn't want to let Mario know that she knew about their relationship so played on him being the big gangster and asked if he knew of any information, she could use to help her brother.

'Your brother is a good kid; we spent a lot of time together last year. He helped me with my girlfriend, she used to like having him around. You know what these girls are like it's cool to have a gay friend—to go shopping with and stuff.'

Jamie cocked her eyebrow and hoped he didn't see it. If that were what he wanted her to believe, she would believe it. Who was she to question someone's morals, she thought?

'He has always spoken highly of you, Mario, and so do a lot of people from the estate. I'm here because I thought that you were maybe—with him that night? And might provide an alibi for him?'

Mario stood up and moved over to the door.

'Sorry Miss Taylor, I don't do alibis. Maybe I was with him, maybe I wasn't. It was a long time ago and I can't remember. Well, it was nice chatting to you—send my regards to your brother.' He opened the door and signalled for his bully boy to come back into the room.

'Please, Mario, you're his last hope. Please...'

They ushered Jamie out of the building. There was no point trying again. She would have to rely on the jury being lenient and hope that Michael could handle himself inside.

Chapter 18

The Magistrates Court was clinically cold, and as Jamie looked around, she could see that half the estate had turned up for the charade of a trial. She had hoped that her mother would be there with Tom but wasn't surprised by her absence. She had refused all contact with her since finding out that it was Michael in the room with her that night. Even Tom had held his tongue in Sheila's defence and not replied to any of Jamie's messages.

Michael stood in the dock in his navy suit and tie. It was not the usual attire for him, and it made him feel even more uncomfortable if that could be possible. The police were still unaware of the events that took place on that evening as he had blatantly refused to answer any of the questions put to him. This would now be a good idea to speak up in light of the hard evidence they had against him; bloodstained clothing that placed him there on the night of the crime was enough for the police to find him guilty, and others were feeling the same.

Judge Margaret Shaw was a stern, short woman. Without hearing her voice, she could have easily been mistaken for a man. As Jamie heard the charges against Michael being read out to him, she gripped Sarah's hand for comfort. She was glad to have her full unconditional support and had fallen completely in love with her. Sarah had told her the same, and the two had become inseparable. Michael looked over to them both and smiled. He was glad that Jamie had someone to look after her. If things didn't go his way and he was to be sent down, at least she wouldn't go off the rails. He had always acted the fool, but he loved his sister unconditionally.

'Michael Taylor, you have been brought before the court in connection with the murder of James Taylor. Allegations have been made against you that on the night in question you did follow your father Mr James Taylor home to the family address that you once resided. This was after an argument that took place earlier in the White Hart Public House. The bloodstains that were found on the carpet suggest that upstairs in your old bedroom you did kill your father then proceed to hide your bloodstained clothes at the back of the wardrobe. When questioned by the police, you have replied in turn with 'no comment' to any of these allegations. This is a preliminary hearing Mr Taylor do you wish to enter a plea at this stage?'

Peter Markham rose to his feet and offered a plea of 'not guilty' for his client. Following this, the judge asked to hear from the state prosecution.

'Thank you, your honour. The body of James Taylor was found several weeks later in the quarry which is situated a few yards from the back of the house that the murder took place. Bloodstains were also found on the path leading to the quarry, and these again after forensic testing were found to be that of the deceased Mr James Taylor. There were also drag marks on the path leading out to the field before the quarry and experts have told us that these may have been caused by the steel toe-cap boots the deceased was wearing. This leads us to believe that after dragging his victim, the defendant later pushed his body into the quarry as if to make it look like an accident.

'The autopsy reports show that he died from a massive trauma to the back of his skull caused by a heavy object and not from drowning.'

The prosecution, a man in his early thirties, seemed so convincing that even Jamie was doubting her brother's innocence as Judge Shaw turned to speak to Michael.

'Mr Taylor, I hope you understand the seriousness of the allegations that have been read out to you. I am now offering you the chance to give your version of events and advise you that a 'no comment' at this stage of the proceedings can only harm your defence, so please take this as sound advice.'

Peter Markham advised Michael to break his silence. With the evidence piling up against him, this was his only chance to gain sympathy from the judge. Michael knew that if she doubted him now, he was sure to go down for murder. He stood in the dock pleading to all that would listen that it was his father that was the monster in all this and not him. He broke his mother's confidence. No more denial. All the years of beatings and mental abuse fell from his quivering lips. He looked over to Jamie and mouthed he was sorry. Sorry for blurting out the Taylor secret in front of her new partner; belittling them both as he told of the abuse they suffered as terrified children and teenagers. He told the court of how his mother had been kept a prisoner for years under his reign of violence and how Jamie and he were raised by an iron fist. He knew that this would mean that his mother had lied on her statement and she would probably never forgive him, but there was no other way; the cards were stacked against him.

Michael almost collapsed after his statement. His face burned red and wet from tears. The judge offered him a glass of water and the state prosecutor asked if they could call their witness.

The Clerk orderly opened the courtroom door and called for Sheila Taylor to take the stand. Jamie and Michael knew nothing about their mother being a witness for the prosecution and were now hoping that she hadn't turned up.

It felt like forever that they left the door open. Then finally, Heather escorted Sheila to the stand as Tom took a chair at the back of the room.

She was sworn in and now standing in the witness box in front of her children. The scars on her face had almost healed, but the scars she suffered on the inside were still clawing away at her as the prosecution questioned her about her police statement.

'Mrs Taylor, the statement you gave to the police is a quite different story to the one that your son has just stated. You say that your husband wasn't setting you on fire but merely helping you away from a fire that you had caused while falling asleep with a cigarette in your mouth. Is this correct?'

Before she could answer Joan Harding, her next-door neighbour for over twenty years shouted out from the public gallery.

'Sheila—tell the truth for the sake of the children. That man was an animal!'

This caused an uproar from the residents of the estate. They all joined in with the woman's plea as Judge Shaw ordered that no comments from the gallery would be tolerated and that any more interruptions and she would have them removed. The prosecution continued.

'Mrs Taylor, please answer the question. You stated that your husband Mr James Taylor was merely helping you, as you had set yourself on fire. Is this correct?'

Sheila asked the Judge for a sip of water and gave her reply.

'No—it's not correct.'

The public gallery broke the silence again and was warned for the last time. Sheila continued.

'He *was* trying to kill me—like he had tried many times before—I didn't know it was Michael at the time, but I knew that someone pulled him off me, and if he hadn't...'

Sheila sobbed profusely. The judge signalled to the clerk to bring her over a chair before confronting her.

'Mrs Taylor, you do realise that you are under oath and that whatever you say now is recorded.'

'Yes, your honour, I want everyone to know the truth. There's no point hiding things anymore. After the fire, I made it down the stairs and out of the door. He was standing at the side of the house holding his bleeding nose. I went over to try to reason with him, then he grabbed my hair and pulled me down to the floor. He kicked me, then walked towards the path to the back of the house. I don't know what came over me. I picked up the car jack that was laying there and then I hit him. With all my last strength, I hit him. I dragged him down to the field, which seemed to take forever, but I did it. Then I rolled him into the water. I watched as he sank to the bottom. For days I thought that I had dreamed it and expected him to walk back through the door, but when he didn't come back I—well anyway, now you all know. It had nothing to do with Mikey. He's a good boy like his dad.'

Sheila looked over to Tom, sat at the back with tears in his eyes.

'Yeah, his dad, Tom Webster, the most kind, considerate man that I have ever met. That's why my husband hated Michael so much, he knew. I spent most of my married life forgiving a man that beat me, raped me, taunted me all because of one drunken carefree night. Which has turned out to have been the best night of my entire life.'

This left Michael bewildered. He had always known deep down that he wasn't a Taylor, and now he had had it confirmed. He was glad that the blood that ran through his veins had nothing to do with the man that he hated more than death itself.

Judge Shaw took off her glasses and rubbed her eyes. The stern, hard-faced woman from before seemed to mellow in her manner. She did not want to continue without Sheila first speaking to a solicitor, but Sheila insisted she wanted to carry on.

'Your Honour, nothing you can do or say will give me more pain than I haven't already been through, a hundred times over. Even if you lock me up and throw away the key, I will still be a free woman. My son Michael and daughter Jamie have been through enough, and it's time I put them first. I can now also put myself first that's why I am not living by his rules anymore. I will cooperate with the police and answer any questions they wish to put to me. Thank you, your honour, that is all I have to say.'

262 ~ KIM HARRY

The courtroom applauded Sheila with the judge's permission.

'Thank you, Mrs Taylor. The police will escort you from the witness box. We will deal with your confession accordingly.'

She told Michael to rise to his feet.

'Mr Michael Taylor, in light of your mother's confession, you are no longer on trial here today and you are now a free man. I wish you all the best for the future and commend you on the bravery and honesty you have shown in this courtroom today, case dismissed.'

* * *

The months that passed seemed a welcome relief in Jamie's eyes. Although her mother was still waiting for a court date, Heather had assured her that all the police callouts over the past twenty years would help her case of diminished responsibility. There were allegations against her father made by others of which Sheila had provided an alibi for, so those would also have to be re-opened and satisfied.

Things were getting back to normal. Michael had started to bond with his newfound father, and although Tom's other children were having a hard time coming to terms with things, they were trying. When they heard that their mother had known about it all along and had forgiven their father for it, it helped. The Webster's marriage had been strong enough to take a few knocks and alcohol had always been a key player in every misdemeanour the family had faced. They had a family rule that they would always blame the drink and not the drinker, so things were forgiven and forgotten.

Jamie had turned thirty, and not as a single woman. She had broken her no relationship rule and Sarah was soon to become the new Mrs Taylor in a civil partnership ceremony, where Sam was to be her 'best woman'. They were now living together as a couple in the house that Jamie owned and soon to become the adoptive parents of a six-week-old baby boy that they had decided to call Ricky. When the papers arrived for them to become his legal guardians, Jamie also signed to legally adopt Molly and their family unit was now complete.

Nothing else mattered to her now but them. She made Michael the entertainments manager of Jewels and promoted Beefy to be his personal bodyguard and caretaker. She knew that Beefy would look after Maud and the other regulars as he had a very thoughtful nature. This took a lot of pressure off her, and she could now take a holiday when needed without the worry of being called back in on a crisis. Michael had always had a soft spot for Beefy and respected his advice, so she knew that he would keep him in check.

She now had the family she had always dreamt of. The past was in the past. There were no ghosts to be afraid of, or guilty secrets to be aired. Heather remained in constant support. She helped Sheila come to terms with the years of suffering that she had endured by her husband and helped her to build a new life for herself with Tom. Jamie was forever grateful to her for helping her mother through such a traumatic time, and they remained close, and that's the way they liked it, as simply good friends.

* * *

Jamie's Story
© 2021 by Kim Harry

ISBN: 978-1-5272-8965-9

Published by Pegbag Publishing.

Thank you for your support.
If you enjoyed this novel, please leave a review on Goodreads and your place of purchase. I read every review and it will help new readers discover my book.
Take Care
Kim x

Lightning Source UK Ltd.
Milton Keynes UK
UKHW041357160521
383816UK00001B/67

9 781527 289659